Glycerine

Garry Ryan

GLYCERINE

A Detective Lane Mystery

NeWest Press

COPYRIGHT © GARRY RYAN 2014

LIBRARY AND ARCHIVES CANADA CATALOGUING IN PUBLICATION

Ryan, Garry, 1953–, author
Glycerine / Garry Ryan.

Issued in print and electronic formats.
ISBN 978-1-927063-68-2 (pbk.).— ISBN 978-1-927063-69-9 (epub).—
ISBN 978-1-927063-70-5 (mobi)

I. Title.

PS8635.Y354G59 2014   C813'.6   C2014-901645-X
                                                                  C2014-901646-8

Editor for the Board: Leslie Vermeer
Cover and interior design: Natalie Olsen, Kisscut Design
Cover photo: (pipeline) © KONG / photocase.com (smoke) © almogon / photocase.com
Author photo: Luke Towers

NeWest Press acknowledges the support of the Canada Council for the Arts, the Alberta Foundation for the Arts, and the Edmonton Arts Council for support of our publishing program. We acknowledge the financial support of the Government of Canada through the Canada Book Fund for our publishing activities.

#201, 8540–109 Street
Edmonton, Alberta T6G 1E6
780.432.9427
NeWest Press www.newestpress.com

No bison were harmed in the making of this book.

Printed and bound in Canada

for
SHARON,
KARMA,
BEN,
LUKE,
INDY,
and
ELLA

✕

After nearly a decade of trying to "kill the Indian" in him, the teachers at Gordon Tootoosis's residential school finally expelled him, according to his daughter Alanna. Her father's transgression: singing powwow with some other students in a music room that Tootoosis and his pals thought was soundproofed. It wasn't. The teachers were outraged when they heard the traditional chanting and singing because it meant that they had failed to transform the kids into docile, English-speaking Roman Catholics.

Obituary of Gordon Tootoosis
Written by Sandra Martin
Globe and Mail
Saturday, July 9, 2011

✕

chapter 1

Father and Brother of Victim Charged in Killing

Shefic Abdula, father of sixteen-year-old Shafina Abdula, and Mohammed Abdula, Shafina's eighteen-year-old brother, have been charged with her murder.

The body of the sixteen-year-old female was discovered in her home on Saturday night. EMS was unable to revive the girl when they arrived at the Abdula home in response to a 911 call.

Shafina was a grade eleven student at Sir John A. Macdonald High School.

Story continues page B3

× 3

chapter 2

"We want you to work with Nigel Li," Harper said.

Lane studied Deputy Chief Cameron Harper before answering. Cam's height and athletic physique filled the office. Behind his black moustache, now sprinkled with grey, his round face was a mask.

Chief Jim Simpson's more delicate features were similarly blank.

Lane looked down at the round table in Harper's office and then at the triangle formed by the chairs they sat in. His eyes focused on the mochaccino in the white paper cup. He could smell the chocolate. *Now it all makes sense.* He looked at Harper and Simpson again and sensed their discomfort.

"Think about it." Simpson wore his uniform jacket with all of the necessary braid. His blond hair was trimmed short.

"For a day." Harper lifted his coffee with hands that made the cup look like a child's.

"We were hoping to hang on to Detective Saliba." Simpson studied Lane's face. "The RCMP wouldn't listen to us. They said that her particular skill set was required elsewhere."

"But we understand why she moved down east to get a fresh start." Harper put his cup down, sat back, and squirmed in his dress uniform.

"And it's important that we continue the process of passing on your skills, your techniques, to a younger detective." Simpson looked sideways at Lane.

Lane was surprised at his annoyance with their use of the word *we* and thought, *Get to the point. Both of you are so worried about following the rules that you've handcuffed yourselves.* "Who is Nigel Li, and what are you holding back?" He raised the mochaccino, took a sip, and smiled. "Don't think you can buy me with one good cup of coffee."

Simpson blinked and smiled. He stood up, loosened his tie, took off his uniform jacket, and hung it on the back of his chair.

Lane spotted the darker blue patches under Chief Simpson's arms.

Harper stood up, took off his jacket, and rolled up his sleeves. "Li is a colossal pain in the ass."

"And a brilliant one. He speaks English, Spanish, and Mandarin." Simpson sat down again and reached for his coffee. He used his left hand to hold back his tie as he sipped.

"So, which is it? Is he brilliant or a pain in the ass?" Lane looked at the liver spots on the backs of his hands.

"Actually, he's both." Simpson smiled as he gauged Lane's reaction.

Before Lane could ask his next question, his phone rang. He raised his hand, pulled the phone from his jacket pocket, and read the name on the display. He looked at the men in front of him. "It's Lori. I have to take this." He pressed a button. "Hello?"

"Tell those two bigwigs that we need you," she said.

Twenty minutes later Lane pulled up behind the Forensic Crime Scene Unit on a residential street. The unit was a white box with ribbon-like blue stripes and a blue-and-white cab up front; its nickname was Big Mac. It was parked out front of a new home being built on an old lot in Hillhurst, one of the more established districts near the river and on the edge of downtown Calgary.

Lane got out of his Chev and walked toward the house. Stepping over a chunk of two-by-six with nails sticking up out of its splintered end, he looked up at the house with its fresh grey coat of stucco. It was two storeys high with a two-car garage around back. A man in a white crime-scene bunny suit stepped out the front door. "You're okay to enter the main level. And the steps into the basement are okay. I'm working on the top level next." He moved aside so the detective could enter.

Lane climbed the front stairs and walked inside where his footsteps echoed on the unfinished floors and uninsulated walls. He followed the familiar stink of rotting meat to the basement door and started downstairs. The steps swayed. They were suspended about a foot from the gravel floor. The wood creaked as he stopped on the bottom step. The concrete walls glowed from the hurricane lamps focused on a spot near the centre of the floor.

A woman in a bunny suit knelt, clearing away gravel with a brush. An ever-expanding section of blue tarp was visible. A man in a matching bunny suit stood behind the woman, videotaping the process.

The kneeling investigator pulled at the tarp to lift away more of the gravel. A bloody hand and forearm came into view, and the stink of rotting meat intensified.

The investigator with the camera stopped, turned, and looked at Lane. The detective met the eyes of the camera operator and recognized him. Lane nodded. "Colin."

Dr. Colin Weaver, the head of the Forensic Crime Scene Unit, was nicknamed Fibre, despite that he was completely unaware of the moniker and equally unaware of the effect his Hollywood face had on women who met him for the first time. "We're just getting started. You're welcome to watch or wait upstairs."

Lane turned and went back to the main floor. He turned left into the kitchen and saw two men sitting on the back step. One had his head shaved so it shone. He wore a red-and-black–checked work shirt and khaki bib overalls. He stared into the backyard and sipped from a stainless-steel thermos.

The other, his back to Lane, had short black hair and wore a blue sportcoat. He talked with his hands, each of which held a paper coffee cup.

Lane turned the doorknob. *Do it quietly and listen,* he thought as he opened the back door.

"So you're saying that the body had to have been buried last night, because you just finished levelling the gravel yesterday afternoon?" the young man with the coffee cups asked.

The man in the work clothes turned to look at Lane. There were lines across his forehead and his brown eyes were weary despite the fact that he looked about eighteen.

"Detective Lane?" The other man turned, stood, and offered a cup to Lane.

Lane asked, "Who are you?"

"Nigel Li." He continued to hold the cup in front of Lane. "Are you going to take it or not? Lori told me what you liked. Don't worry, it's still hot."

Lane took the cup, held it close to his nose, smelled the chocolate, and took a sip. "Perfect." *Does everyone think they get on my good side by buying me a mochaccino?* He took another sip. *They're probably right.*

"She said it would be a good icebreaker," Nigel said.

Lane took a close look at Nigel's freckled round face, unruly black hair, and brown eyes. He stood easily six foot two. Lane offered his hand, and Nigel took it with a smile. *He looks relieved,* Lane thought.

Nigel glanced at the man in the work clothes. "This is Jim. He discovered the body."

Lane looked at Jim, who stood up and offered his hand. Lane felt the calluses on Jim's hand as their palms and fingers gripped.

Nigel continued. "He says he finished up work at about six o'clock last night, then came to check on the job this morning before the concrete was poured. He noticed that . . ."

Lane thought, *However you react, it will probably make or break your relationship with Nigel.* He put his hand on Nigel's shoulder. The young officer gave Lane a puzzled look. Lane smiled at Nigel, then turned his attention to Jim.

Jim stared into the backyard.

Lane sat down on the step and waited for Jim to do the same.

Nigel stepped down onto the dirt. He watched the older detective and the witness.

Lane glanced up at Nigel, then looked to see what Jim was staring at. He saw that the garage door was open. There was darkness behind the open door.

"Do you know who it is?" Jim's eyes turned away from the garage.

"Not yet," Lane said.

Jim nodded, looked at Lane, and sat down next him. "I finished up levelling off the basement last night. This morning I could tell someone had been there afterward. I went to level the floor again. That's when my rake hooked on an eye at the corner of the tarp. There was that smell. It's been so hot lately, and it was hot in there yesterday."

Nigel opened his mouth.

Lane silenced him with a glance, a slight shake of the head, and a smile.

"I saw his face. His eyes were wide open." Jim focused on Lane. "He's from Mexico, right?"

"At this moment, you know more than I do," Lane said.

Jim nodded and turned back to staring at the shadow behind the open garage door. "Mexican. Some of the Latino guys come up here to work construction."

Lane glanced at Nigel, who appeared to be intently studying the conversation.

"When I lifted the tarp, I caught a glimpse of his face. His mouth was open. So were his eyes. I dropped the tarp and went back upstairs. Called 911 from my cell phone." Jim turned to Lane. "From the look on his face, he died in agony."

×

Fibre pulled back his hood and said, "It's going to be hot today. I'll get the results of the autopsy and our other findings to you as soon as they come to me." He turned his back on the detectives and walked toward the cab of the FCSU vehicle.

Lane got into the Chev, waited for Nigel to do the same, and watched the van pull away.

"How come you did that?" Nigel asked.

"Did what?" He heard a measure of defensiveness in Nigel's tone, but it was overshadowed by curiosity.

"You put your hand on my shoulder to stop me talking." Nigel looked forward.

He's asking you a direct question. Give him a direct answer. "I got the feeling he was ready to talk, so I put my hand on your shoulder to give him that opportunity."

Nigel nodded. "I do have a bad habit of saying too much."

Now see what he thinks. "I have a habit of saying too little. What impressions did you get from the scene and from Jim?"

Nigel regarded Lane with a hint of disbelief. "You want my opinion?"

Lane waited.

"The victim was killed elsewhere and wrapped in the tarp. The killer — I'm assuming it was a he because of the size of the body and the strength required to carry it into the basement — looked for a place to dump the body where it wouldn't be found. The location was probably picked at random. It's close to a major traffic artery so it's a reasonable assumption that he turned off of Crowchild Trail and found a house with a basement floor waiting to be poured. If Fibre's initial finding is correct, then the victim was probably shot in the back with a hunting rifle. The enlarged exit wound is consistent with that." Nigel crossed his arms as if he were preparing for Lane to lecture him.

You sound very sure of yourself, but your body language contradicts that, Lane thought.

The street was heavily treed, and they moved in and out of shade as they headed for Crowchild Trail. Nigel watched the bicycle traffic rolling along between the Chev and the sidewalk. A young woman rode a neon-green bike with wide handle bars. Her skirt was tucked between her knees. She wore a neon-green helmet and sunglasses. "Do you ride a bike?"

Lane shook his head. "I walk a dog."

"What kind of dog?" They slowed and stopped for a red light. The woman on the bike passed them on the right.

"She's a mutt," Lane said.

"Like me," Nigel said.

"Me too."

"No, not like me. Look at that!" Nigel pointed at a black pickup truck travelling north on Crowchild Trail. The truck had a semi's cab, a pickup's box, and tires that would fit a tractor. The vehicle stood at least three metres high. "Now there's dumbspicuous consumption."

"What?" Lane asked.

"You know, conspicuous consumption that's dumb." Nigel turned and held his earlobe, then pointed at Lane. "What happened to yours?"

"Violent spouse in a domestic dispute," Lane said.

Nigel nodded. "A lot of that going around."

✕

"You'd better be nice to him." Lori sat behind her computer monitor and shook her finger at Lane. She was the detectives' blonde receptionist and something of a mother to them all. "Some of those so-called tough guys gave him a rough ride.

Just between you and me, I think they thought Nigel should shut up and do as he was told. The problem is, he has a mind of his own." She leaned closer. "And he's quicker than all of them."

Lane opened his mouth, closed it, and indicated that he had surrendered by turning his palms up.

"Nigel is smart. I know he talks a lot, but he has a lot to say if you take the time to listen." Lori stood up, continued to wag her finger, and smiled. She wore a black dress, red cowboy boots, a black Stetson, glasses with rainbow frames, and real freshwater pearls. "So you'll have to tangle with me if I hear that you're giving Nigel a rough time. The kid hasn't had it easy, you know."

"What do you mean?" *What's the story here?*

Lori cocked her head to the right. "Not my place to say."

"So I'm supposed to fly blind on this one?" Lane took a long breath and shook his head.

"You're the detective. Do a little digging. I can't do all of the work around here." She winked at Lane and raised a pink bottle of bubble solution. "If you're nice, I might even blow a few bubbles your way." The phone rang. She smiled, winking at him, and turned to answer it.

Lane walked to his office. He had an office of his own since being promoted and put in charge of major crimes. He soon found the promotion meant more headaches to go along with a wee bit more money after taxes.

He sat down behind his computer and looked at the family photograph of his partner Arthur, nephew Matt, niece Christine, her boyfriend Daniel, and Roz the dog.

He logged in and checked his police service e-mail, then switched to his personal account. Spotting Keely Saliba's name, Lane opened a message.

From: Keely Saliba (janebond@cmail.com)
Sent: July 08, 9:28:40 AM
To: Lane (PLane@cmail.com)
CC: Cam Harper (cam.harper@cmail.com)

Re: UPDATE

Lane,

Sorry it took so long to get back to you.

I like my new job, and I'm one of the lucky ones who gets to work with some really talented individuals. And, as usual, they know how to get the job done despite the way the system works. The problem is that they all work hard, and I have to work harder to catch up.

Dylan loves law school here. I think it's not that he loves the school so much; it's more likely the result of us moving three thousand kilometres from my father. The problem is we miss so many other people who are still in Calgary.

You must be wondering if I'll ever get to the point. I have a favour to ask. There have been some unusual incidents in your city. When the government isn't threatening us with being thrown out of the intelligence business, it's ordering us to actively share information with CSIS and other agencies. I got this tip because I have Calgary connections. Apparently sales of glycerine are up in Cowtown, especially in the northwest. Also, fifty litres of sulphuric acid were stolen from a chrome-plating business in the southeast. Nothing else was touched including some cash in the secretary's desk. If there is a similar theft of nitric acid, you may have trouble headed your way. Of course you know that glycerine, sulphuric acid, and nitric acid are used to produce nitroglycerine.

It appears that you and I are destined to deal with explosives. Just keep me in the loop if any news about these ingredients comes your way.

Oh, and I've used your personal e-mail addresses just in case there are any Scotch drinkers hacking into your work accounts. I guess old habits really do die hard.

Keely

"You're not going to leave him back there in those cubicles, are you?" Lori stood in the doorway with the index finger of her right hand pointed at him. She tipped her Stetson back with a thumb. She looked from left to right at the expanse of his office. "There's room for two desks in here."

"What are you talking about?" Lane looked around his new office. *Oh shit. I just got comfortable here. What is she planning?*

Lori stepped inside the office and closed the door behind her. "Nigel doesn't fit back there with the good ol' boys and girls. Most of them still think Smoke was a great chief. You and I both know it was because he promised each of them some kind of promotion down the road. He made those promises with no intention of ever following through with them." She frowned at Lane and crossed her arms.

Lane recognized the significance of her crossed arms. *Uh-oh. When she does that, either I'm about to hear bad news or she already has her mind made up about something.* "And?"

"I think Nigel should move in here with you."

"Ohh." Lane took a long breath.

"So, it's okay with you if I get another desk moved in here today?" Lori crossed her right boot over her left and leaned her back up against the door. The implication was clear: she wasn't leaving until Lane went along with her plan.

"Do I have any choice?" Lane asked.

"Of course not." Lori opened the door, then turned to face him. "There's a red file folder on my desk. It contains articles and court documents. You need to read them. Just to make your job a little easier." The heels of Lori's boots announced her departure.

×

Donna Laughton stood on an upturned plastic milk crate as she tightened up the last of eight spark plugs. She grabbed a loose wire, then snapped the wire onto the top of the plug. "Now you'd better run, you son of a bitch." Her garage smelled of grease, gasoline, and decomposing automobile.

Donna backed out from under the white hood of her panel van and stepped down from the crate. Leaning back, she put her fists against the small of her spine. She closed her eyes and turned her neck to work out the inevitable kinks resulting from contorting herself to operate within the van's cramped engine compartment. She gathered her tools to return them to their various drawers in her red Snap-on toolbox. Donna checked the knuckles of her right hand, saw a flap of skin, and sucked at the blood of a skinned knuckle. She grimaced at the taste of blood mixed with motor oil.

After she walked around the side of the van, Donna undid the front of her blue coveralls, wiggled them down over her shoulders, and let them fall around her knees. The hinges on the van's door complained as she opened it and sat down on the floor. She worked her feet out of the coveralls and hung them over the top of the door.

She hauled her compact frame into the seat. The seat back was angled at about fifty degrees. Donna turned the key. The engine coughed, then caught.

She let the engine idle while she climbed out and walked alongside the van, careful not to rub her grey T-shirt against the rust that was working its way along the side panel. Donna reached for the garage door opener and tapped the button.

When the door opened, she looked at the second panel van. It was grey and ready for its trip up the hill into the district across John Laurie Boulevard. She looked over the roof of the van. The cream stuccoed walls and red-tiled roof of the Eagle's Nest Christian Church looked down on the houses of Donna's neighbourhood. The church's sign proclaimed:

GOD THE SON
GOD THE FATHER
GOD THE HOLY SPIRIT
THE ONE TRUE GOD

You bastards don't understand that this is how wars start! Donna thought. She looked to her right and down the street. A ten-minute walk from her house was the Ranchlands Islamic Centre, located in a strip mall across from the Catholic school. "Maybe we can put a stop to this war of words."

"Sorry?" a man said.

Again she looked to her right. The man stood on the sidewalk. Donna recognized him immediately. Standing six foot one and weighing about one hundred and eighty pounds, the man wore a neatly trimmed black beard with a hint of grey and had handsome yet nondescript features — except of course for the missing chunk of earlobe. His companion, an Australian cattle dog mixed with border collie, was predominantly black with some tan on its belly and a white patch at its throat. Donna smiled. "Just talking to myself. How's Roz this evening?"

Lane smiled back. "Raring to go."

She watched Roz drag him past the grey panel van, down the sidewalk, and across the street. *What is that guy's name?*

Donna went back inside the garage to shut off the van. As she closed the door, she looked at the cases of glycerine stacked against the wall. Above the cases was a picture of her sister Lisa wearing a beret, a camouflage jacket, and a smile.

✕

Lane opened the front door, bent to unclip Roz's leash, wiped her paws, and slipped out of his shoes. Roz scampered for a drink of water.

Lane looked into the living room. Arthur sat with his feet tucked up on the couch. His generous belly curved above the elastic waist of his black yoga pants.

"Hello, Lane." Next-door neighbour Maria sat dwarfed by the chair-and-a-half that lounged in front of the windows. Her strawberry-blonde hair was cut short, and she held her right hand atop a five-month baby bump.

"How are you feeling?" Lane asked.

"The baby kicked today." Maria smiled.

Lane sat down in the easy chair. *When we first met you were wearing something from Victoria's Secret, locked out of the house with lasagna in the oven.* "That's exciting."

Arthur put his feet on the floor. "She's worried about what happened at the Islamic Centre."

Lane turned to Maria. "What happened?"

"Somebody fired paintballs at the windows."

"So things aren't cooling off," Lane said.

"Not since the murder in Hawkwood." Arthur pointed with his finger in the general direction of the neighbourhood to the north.

"The father and brother have been charged," Lane said.

"I know," Maria said. "Apparently, the minister at the Eagle's Nest Christian Church has been stirring up the congregation."

"And the family of the murdered girl are members of the Islamic Centre?" Lane asked.

Maria nodded.

"I wasn't involved in that investigation or the arrest. I do know that the father and brother confessed at the scene." Lane heard a key in the front-door lock.

Roz barked, the front door opened, and Christine stepped

inside, followed by Daniel. She was six foot two; he, six five. They were the tallest people in the house.

"How was the movie?" Arthur asked.

Christine rolled her eyes, kicked off her pumps, and bent to greet Roz. "How's my baby?"

"She didn't like the movie," Dan said.

Christine stood, pushed back her black hair, spotted Maria, and stepped closer to give her a hug. "How are you feeling?"

"Finished with the nausea. Finally." Maria stood up. Her head didn't quite reach Christine's chin.

Turning back to Arthur and Lane, Maria continued, shrugging her shoulders. "I'm just worried about what's happening in this neighbourhood. Feelings are running high, and I think paintball guns are an escalation."

"Paintball guns?" Christine asked.

"Someone shot paintballs at the Islamic Centre," Arthur said.

Lane looked at Arthur. "I'll see what I can find out."

"Where's Matt?" Dan asked.

"Asleep," Arthur said.

"He's turning into a hermit," Christine said.

Dan tried to smile, looked at Lane, and frowned. "He really is, you know."

✕

Chris Jones pushed the vacuum back and forth on the carpet. As the machine heated up, it smelled of burnt rubber and singed dust.

He was working in the corner of the president's office, which was situated at the front end of the eight-thousand-square-foot building that housed Foothills Fertilizers. Chris smiled at the way the plush pale carpet revealed his work with subtly different shades of blue where the vacuum left its mark.

Chris looked at his watch, shut off the vacuum, listened for the sounds of other human activity, and undid the buttons on the cuffs of his shirt.

He watched his watch work its way to exactly ten o'clock. The desk phone rang.

Chris waited for three rings before he picked up the receiver with his right hand, which he'd covered with the fabric of his cuff. "Christopher." If he had said, "Chris Jones," it meant they were not free to talk.

"How are things?" John A. Jones asked.

An insight struck Chris like a camera's flash in total darkness. *His voice. It's God's voice,* he thought. "I'm good."

"The inventory is complete?" his father asked.

"Almost." Chris felt himself begin to shrink inside his two-hundred-twenty-pound frame.

"Almost?"

Chris reacted to the disappointment, the note of accusation in the one-word question. "One more litre, and the inventory will be complete."

"Good. The deadline is approaching. The only way to win this war is to bring the battle to the city that creates the filth," John A. intoned.

"I understand." Chris patted the muffin top over his belt.

"God will protect us."

"He will."

"Your mother sends her love," John A. said.

Chris frowned and thought, *My mother is dead.* "I know."

"I will call again tomorrow night."

Chris hung up, did up his sleeves, and restarted the vacuum.

×

Matt blinked in the darkness and stared at the luminous dial of the alarm clock.

He kept his eyes open as he swung his legs off the bed and walked to the light switch. He looked at his toes when he turned on the light.

With the palm of his hand, he touched the sheen of sweat on his chest. He closed his eyes and again saw the man in the devil mask, felt the cold of devil's handgun against his forehead.

He opened his eyes and headed for the bathroom and a shower. *It's ninety minutes before I have to be at the golf course*, he thought as he opened the bathroom cupboard and looked for a fresh towel.

chapter 3

Christian Woman Sentenced to Death for Blasphemy

Rassima Abdula is set to die after being found guilty of blaspheming the Prophet Mohammed. She was accused of insulting the prophet while arguing with a neighbour.

The forty-year-old mother of five was convicted in a Pakistan court after spending two years in jail awaiting a court date.

Rahim Abdula, her eldest son, who is a Canadian citizen living in Calgary, told reporters, "My mother was unjustly accused. Now she has been unjustly sentenced."

Amnesty International has called for Rassima's sentence to be overturned on the basis that there was only one witness to the crime. The unnamed accuser has been in a long-standing dispute with Abdula over a parcel of land.

Rassima has become a cause célèbre for North American evangelical Christian groups, who say her conviction is an attack on fundamental religious freedoms.

Professor Richard Finn of the University of Calgary's Religious Studies Department says, "The Rassima Abdula case has increased fears in some of the faithful. Unfortunately, extremists on both sides are quick to exploit these fears."

Lane cracked two eggs on the edge of the sink and dropped them into the frying pan. A pair of orangey-yellow yolks stared back at him.

"What are you doing up this early?" Matt stepped into the kitchen. His face, neck, and arms were tanned from working six days out of seven on the golf course.

"Want some breakfast?" Lane asked. *Matt, you're losing weight.*

"Sure." Matt shrugged.

"Scrambled?"

"Please." Matt poured two cups of coffee. "You didn't answer my question."

Lane struggled to grab hold of a nagging image in a shadowy corner of his mind. "It's parade day. I like to get downtown before the Stampede crowd. It gives me time for a cup of coffee and a look around."

Matt sat down at the table, sipped his coffee, and rubbed his right palm across his eyes.

"Nightmare?" Lane grabbed the flipper and turned the eggs.

The toast popped out of the toaster. Matt hopped up on one leg to butter it. "Can we talk about something else?"

Let it go or face the problem head on? "No. You've lost weight, there are dark circles under your eyes, and you're not yourself."

"Shit! I don't have time for this. I'm going to work." Matt dropped the knife, walked to the front door, shoved his feet into his shoes, grabbed his jacket, and went outside.

Lane lifted the eggs, turned them, and arranged them on the toast. The yolky yellow eyes accused him of being a failure as a parent. He sat down to eat. *This isn't entirely unexpected. He survived the kidnapping, and the scars are showing. I need to call Dr. Alexandre on the way to work this morning.*

Fifty minutes later he had a mochaccino in his hand and was sitting on a bench next to the bronze statues of the Famous Five: five memorable women who'd fought for women to be recognized as persons and — as a result — able to vote in Canada. On parade mornings Lane often sat across from the Five and watched the performers on their way to the parade. *It's better than the actual Stampede Parade. I never know what to expect. And there is an unrehearsed quality to it.*

Across from him, the Centre for the Performing Arts looked down on Stephen Avenue.

The clop of hooves made Lane look east. Two police officers wearing blue uniforms and black Stetsons rode up the Avenue on a pair of black geldings. Behind them, two First Nations women rode a pair of palominos whose coats looked like gold in the morning light. Their graceful passing was made more fluid by the reflected images of the women in the windows of the Centre. The women had their hair braided at the back and wore handmade costumes beaded with red and turquoise. Both horses stopped as the nearest one lifted its tail and dropped a bushel of road apples. The stink rose up from the steaming pile and wafted its way downwind.

Next came kilted men holding bagpipes. The heels of their boots made a unified crunch as the pipers marched as one entity. Even their kilts swayed in unison. The red Glengarry caps had red pompoms on top that bobbed each time their heels contacted the pavement.

A jogger followed the pipers. The man wore sweatpants and a grey T-shirt and had green fabric wrapped around his hands. He stopped in front of one of the performing arts centre windows and began to shadow box.

Lane studied the boxer, who turned and again began to follow the pipers.

"Nigel?" Lane asked.

Nigel looked in Lane's direction, smiled, and waved. He crossed the avenue, all the while wrapping and unwrapping the tape on his left hand. "You're here early."

"We both are."

"I like to take a run on the days I fight." Nigel sat down next to Lane.

"Fight?" Lane nodded at Nigel's hands.

"I box every other Friday night."

"Boxing? Isn't that a little tough on the brain?" Lane asked.

"We wear head gear."

"I don't get it. It doesn't seem like something I'd imagine you doing."

"It's hard to explain," Nigel said.

Lane waited.

"I've got a busy mind." Nigel tapped the side of his head with his taped right hand. "Boxing gives me a rest from all of those thoughts running around inside. I have to concentrate on other things. Elemental things."

"Oh." *It still doesn't make a lot of sense to me.*

"Don't worry, my friends don't understand it either."

"What about your family?" Lane asked.

"My mother is dead, and my father is in prison. I have no siblings." Nigel resumed unravelling the tape on his left hand.

Lane heard the desolation in Nigel's voice and decided to stop asking questions.

"It's a real conversation stopper, isn't it?" Nigel said as if in apology. He switched to the tape on his right hand.

"I walk the dog or run with the geese to clear my mind."

Nigel turned to stare at his new partner. "Run with the geese?"

"Ever been at the big soccer fields at Shouldice Park?"

Nigel shook his head.

You must think you've been partnered with a madman. "It's a trick my nephew showed me. A flock of geese often grazes on the grass near the river. If you run into the flock, they take off and it makes you feel like you're flying. And whatever is bothering you leaves with the geese. It's kind of —"

"— cathartic," Nigel said.

"You have an annoying habit of —"

"— completing people's sentences for them." Nigel stood up. "Got to finish my run and hit the shower."

Lane watched Nigel run west along the avenue. He hopped over the pile of road apples and shadow boxed the odious air.

Lane's phone rang. He reached into his pocket and pulled out the phone. "Lane."

"I've been expecting a call from you. Your nephew Matt is experiencing difficulty?"

Lane set his coffee down when he recognized the voice. "Dr. Alexandre. Thank you for returning my call so quickly."

"I read about what happened to your nephew. Often, after an experience like that, there are residual issues. When can I see him?" Dr. Alexandre asked.

Lane began to sweat. "I haven't asked him yet. I wanted to make sure that you were available before I broached the subject with Matt."

"He's having trouble sleeping, he's losing weight, and he's becoming socially withdrawn?" Alexandre asked.

"That's correct." *Now there are two people finishing my thoughts for me.*

"I'll let the receptionist know that Matt gets a blue space. It means Matt will get in quicker. Just remember that I said fill in a blue space when you phone the appointment in," Alexandre said.

"Thank you."

"The sooner we get started, the better for everyone concerned." Alexandre hung up.

An hour later, Lane was sitting in front of his computer. Lori knocked on the door. "Did you check?"

Lane looked up from the screen.

Lori stood in a long floral-print skirt and a white blouse. She leaned against the doorframe, one red cowboy boot crossed in front of the other.

"Check what?" Lane's computer chirped as a new e-mail message arrived.

"I thought so." Lori turned. Her skirt flared. "I'm sending you an e-mail, and I'll be checking back with you in fifteen minutes to see whether you've read it."

Lane listened to her boots pounding down the hall as he looked at his screen. The new message was from Fibre. Lane was probably the only officer on the force who knew that Fibre was the father of triplets.

The message was direct, as always, with three items:

FOUND IN WATCH POCKET OF SUBJECT'S JEANS:
1. Receipt from Crowfoot Cinema
2. Receipt from Crowfoot Pharmacy
3. Receipt from Post Office

Copies of three receipts and a photo of the subject are attached.

The subject was killed approximately ten hours before burial.
The subject was buried for approximately four hours before being discovered. Grease, hydraulic fluid, bituminous sand, alfalfa, oat straw, and sweet clover were found on his clothing. Bullet fragments were retrieved from the chest cavity and are being processed.

Lane studied the message for a moment, opened the attachments, then printed two copies of each receipt and the photograph. He stapled one, labelled it for Nigel, then folded the others and stuffed them into his jacket pocket.

There was a knock on his door. He looked up at a man wearing blue work clothes. The man's head was shaved, and he had tigers tattooed on either side of his scalp just above the ears. Lane got up and opened the door.

"You ordered a desk?"

×

Donna put on her red helmet, zipped up her red leather jacket, pulled on her red gloves, gripped the clutch with her left hand, and touched the starter with her right thumb.

The sound of the Harley Davidson Superlow's engine filled the garage with its rumbling, thundering power. Donna shifted into gear, released the clutch, and eased her way out of the garage, down the driveway, and over the curb.

She left the neighbourhood and opened up the throttle as she drove along John Laurie Boulevard. On her right, a group of men stood beneath the Eagle's Nest Christian Church sign that looked down on the roadway.

ALLAH THE ONE TRUE GOD

Donna throttled back as she passed the men and women. She saw one bearded man pointing at the sign. His cheeks and forehead were red. She couldn't hear what he said but could tell that his mouth was spewing rage.

She passed the clutch of followers and accelerated as the red light up ahead turned green.

Five minutes later she was on the four-lane highway headed west. The sky was dotted with cumulus clouds. Their lazy eastward progress cast shadows over the Rockies. This morning the mountains seemed closer than usual, magnified by some atmospheric effect.

Traffic was light because so many people had slept in or taken the morning off instead of going to the parade. She cruised at one hundred kilometres per hour. The wind tugged at her clothing, and a dragonfly smacked against her face shield.

It was at times like this that Donna found she had her best conversations with Lisa. The full-face helmet meant she didn't have to explain why she was talking to her dead twin sister. The open road, the Rockies, and the wind made her feel free to say what was on her mind.

"Still think that motorbike is better than having a man between your legs?" Lisa asked.

"Yes." Donna smiled.

"I know that Steve was a drunk and a chauvinist, but they're not all like that."

"Can we talk about something else?" Donna asked.

"Okay! Let's talk about your big plans for a week from today."

"If you like."

"You don't sound all that happy about it."

"Well, you already told me that you think I'm nuts to do it, so there's really no point in trying to talk me out of it." Donna checked her side mirror as a black pickup truck pulled up close behind her. She looked ahead. The left lane was open. The driver of the pickup could easily pass her if he wanted.

"The plan sounds fine. I'm just worried about the consequences. Unexpected consequences. People don't always react the way you expect them to. There's no such thing as a perfect plan."

Donna looked in her mirror. The truck driver smoked a cigarette and eased closer. Now she could see only the truck's grille in her mirror.

"Go ahead and deal with that asshole. I'll wait," Lisa said.

Donna took her left hand off the handlebars and reached into her jacket pocket. She gripped a handful of steel ball bearings the size of marbles. She held her left fist down low, below her hip. Donna checked ahead and behind in her mirror to ensure there was no other traffic nearby. Then she opened her fist. The metal balls bounced on the pavement. She heard the crack of steel meeting metal, plastic, and glass.

"Is he giving you some space?" Lisa asked.

Donna watched the truck shrink in her mirror. "Yes."

"You never saw what I saw in Afghanistan. What people are capable of. And people do violence with explosives and guns as calmly as you did just now when you dropped those metal balls on the pavement."

"You think I don't know that? I did experience the damage one man can do to your mind, to your soul." Donna eased off the throttle when she approached the eighty-kilometre-per-hour limit where the highway began its descent into the river valley. The mountains were in her face now.

"I saw kids, toddlers, killed in some of the explosions."

"A sixteen-year-old girl was killed just up the hill from my house. Her father and brother are charged with the killing. I know all about people and violence." Donna downshifted as the road's angle of decline increased. She could see part of the town of Cochrane settled on the floodplain nestled in a U of the Bow River.

"Don't believe everything you see on the news. It's not reality."

"Oh, but it shapes reality. It starts people talking. Then the words turn into anger between people of different religions. They always go after one another with their angry words first — then somebody gets hurt." Donna leaned into the first curve.

"So you're saying I was killed because of words? Let me tell you, that blast didn't feel like words."

Donna nodded as she leaned into the next curve and saw more of Cochrane in the valley on her left. "That's what I'm saying. I'm saying you *can* connect the words to the violent actions."

"You don't think that's a bit of an oversimplification?"

Donna thought for a little while as she downshifted and slowed to fifty kilometres per hour. "Sure it is, but it's also true. First come the words. Then comes the violence. It's that simple." She flicked on her turn indicator, then turned left into the town. When she reached Main Street, she turned left again and parked across the street from MacKay's Ice Cream. She shut the engine off, lowered the kickstand, leaned the bike over, and swung her right leg over the saddle. Then she lifted off her helmet and ran her fingers through her light-brown hair. She crossed the street and stood in front of the ice cream shop. Sweet scents of all of the creamy flavours wafted out the front door. A three-year-old boy wore a chocolate moustache as he focused on devouring a treat before it could melt onto his hand.

Tires screamed as a vehicle braked.

Donna turned and reflexively took one step toward the street.

"Hey you! Motorcycle bitch!" said a man with a black ball cap, a goatee, and his left hand pointing a cigarette from the window of his black pickup truck. It stood about a metre off the ground on oversized tires.

Donna stood her ground and eyed her assailant.

"Ya, you! What the fuck did you do to my truck?" He took a drag from his cigarette.

Donna took a moment to reply. She glanced at the people on the sidewalk who had stopped to watch. The father of the three-year-old stood up. The little boy looked up from his ice cream, then stuck his tongue and nose back into the chocolate.

"Do you want an ice cream?" Donna asked.

"No, I don't want a fucking ice cream!" the driver said.

Donna shrugged and waited. *Now you have a decision to make, macho boy.* She looked around her as people began to focus on the driver. She also noted the way they frowned. Some were spectators, some began to walk away, and others were placing themselves between the trucker and their children. One mother picked a cell phone out of her purse and started tapping in numbers. A sixteen-year-old girl held up her phone to capture the action.

Donna stepped down from the sidewalk and onto the pavement.

"I'm coming after you!" The driver revved his engine and began to roll forward.

Donna took another step closer.

"Back off, bitch!" The driver moved further down Main Street.

Donna stepped out between parked cars.

The truck was half a block away. The driver gave her a one-finger salute. "This ain't over!" He shifted gears and the engine raced. The rear tires smoked when he turned left.

Donna turned and walked into MacKay's. After buying a lemon sorbet, she sat outside and savoured the treat. Ten minutes later, she got back on her motorcycle. She turned onto the highway and headed back toward the city. The engine roared as she began the long climb up from Cochrane and out of the Bow River Valley.

"Aren't you afraid he'll be waiting for you?" Lisa asked.

Donna shook her head. "Nope."

"You'll handle it either way?" Lisa asked.

"I learned it from you. You stood up to Steve when you moved me out of his house. It took me a while to realize that he nearly took my soul away. I was so afraid of him that I would do whatever I had to do to keep him from beating on me. You gave me back what I'd lost. Once I got that back, I could control the fear rather than have it control me. You must have noticed that he kept moving away as I moved closer to him. You taught me to pay attention to things like that." Donna crested the hill and accelerated to one hundred kilometres per hour.

"So little sister is standing on her own two feet."

"That's right. And remember you're only twelve minutes older than me." Donna breathed deep, looked ahead, and saw an open stretch of road. She twisted the throttle and held on with her thighs as the Superlow leapt forward. Ahead she could see the golden stacks of the gas extraction plant.

Back in the city, driving along John Laurie Boulevard, she saw a man on a ladder placing new letters on the sign at the Eagle's Nest Church. A woman stood on the bottom rung of the ladder and said something to the man that made him look down at her.

Donna read the new message.

DON'T JUST SAY YOU BELIEVE IN GOD KNOW HIM IN JESUS CHRIST

Donna thought, *It always begins with words.*

✕

"Thanks for letting me move into your office." Nigel dropped a box beside the new computer on the metal desk across from Lane's.

"Lori put in a good word for you." Lane leaned back in his chair.

Nigel picked up the copies of the receipts on his desk. "What are these?"

"Receipts found on yesterday's body." Lane looked at the copies on his desk.

Nigel flipped through the receipts. "We gotta go!"

"What?" Lane asked.

"We need to find a post office in the area." Nigel turned and stepped to the door.

"I don't follow." Lane stood and grabbed his sports jacket.

"The guys from Mexico usually go to the post office on their day off to mail money orders back home. If you look at the receipt you see that the post office and pharmacy have the same address. People who know the victim will probably be at the post office this morning because almost everyone gets time off work to go to the Stampede Parade." Nigel held the door open for Lane.

Lane grabbed the photo and receipts from his desk and hurried out of the door.

Lori raised her eyebrows as they rushed past her. Before the detectives could leave the office, she asked, "Did you read my e-mail, Detective Lane?"

Lane heard the ominous tone in her voice. "When I get back."

It took half an hour to get to the northwest corner of the city where a patchwork of pastel-coloured strip malls sold everything from shoes to gourmet cupcakes. The parking lot was big enough to house a covered football stadium.

"You live around here, don't you?" Nigel waited to make a left turn near the liquor store whose advertising recommended an evening of old Scotch, fine wine, and prairie oysters in honour of the Stampede. Nigel crossed another intersection.

"Turn right here." Lane pointed.

Nigel parked in front of Double Value Drugs. In the window hung the blue-and-red Canadian post office logo.

As they climbed out of the Chev, Nigel took off his jacket and holster. "Will you hold onto this for me?" He held out his Glock.

"What are you doing?"

"You know how Mexicans react to the police, don't you?" Nigel closed the driver's door.

"No." Lane tucked the weapon into the pocket of his grey sports jacket.

"In Mexico, you stay clear of the police whenever possible."

Lane closed his door, moved around the front of the car, and tapped his jacket pocket. "How do you know?"

"When I was a kid, my parents had a condo in Cancun. We used to go there for a month every winter." Nigel walked through the automatic door.

Inside the store, Lane pointed. "On your left at the back."

Lane followed Nigel to the back of the store where five men stood in line at the counter. A harried clerk of no more than sixteen helped a woman fill out a form so that she could send her parcel to Asia.

Nigel looked at Lane. "Hang back."

Lane turned red and glared at his partner.

"No offence." Nigel blushed and leaned his head in the direction of the Latino men waiting in line.

Lane went to stand near the potato chips and cheezies. He watched as Nigel walked up to the first man in line. He was dressed in jeans and a green T-shirt.

Nigel asked, "*Señor?*"

It was the only word in the conversation that Lane understood.

Nigel showed the man in the green T-shirt the picture. The man shook his head and said, "No."

Lane watched for ninety minutes as Nigel talked to

Mexican workers who were handing over wads of cash to be sent to relatives in Mexico.

The line thinned out. Nigel waited. Now there was no one in line. Nigel frowned at his partner. Lane went to the front of the store and looked outside.

Lane recognized a man with a purple shirt who had been in line thirty minutes ago. Two men approached the man in the purple shirt. He said something to the men. They nodded and returned the way they had come.

Lane walked back to the post office counter and tapped Nigel on the shoulder. "I need you to interpret for me while I talk with a fellow."

Nigel followed Lane outside where the older detective stood in front of the man with the purple shirt.

"What are you doing?" Nigel asked Lane.

Lane held up his hand to indicate that Nigel should wait. Lane studied the man in the purple shirt, whose eyes were fixed on his white running shoes. He'd stuffed his hands in the pockets of his jeans.

Lane looked at the thick black hair atop the man's head. Lane turned to Nigel and said, "Tell him that I will arrest him for interfering with a police investigation if he doesn't tell us what he knows about the man in the picture."

"What?" Nigel asked.

Lane glared at Nigel.

Nigel began to speak to the man in the purple shirt, who lifted his round face and brown eyes only once to look first at Nigel, then at Lane.

"Oscar Mendes," the man in the purple shirt said.

Nigel asked, "*¿Cómo se llama?*"

The man in the purple shirt said, "Miguel."

"*¿Qué sabe usted de los premios Oscar,*" Nigel said.

Miguel began to talk. The words fell out rapidly. Lane caught the odd word like *blanco* and *grande*.

When Miguel was done, Nigel asked Lane, "Anything you want to ask him?"

"Just his phone number if we need to get in touch with him."

Nigel asked, "*¿Cuál es su número telefónico.*"

Miguel told him and Nigel tapped the number into his cell phone.

"Anything else?" Nigel asked.

Lane handed Miguel his card.

Miguel looked at Lane, who said, "*Gracias.*"

Nigel chuckled. Miguel smiled.

"What?" Lane asked.

"Your Spanish accent is horrible," Nigel said.

Five minutes later, Lane and Nigel sat under the trellis at a local coffee shop. Potted plants bloomed in reds and blues in a wooden half-barrel next to their table. A cowboy twirling a lasso was painted on the glass beside them.

Nigel took a sip of his vanilla latte. "Miguel thought we were looking for illegal immigrants, and he was warning the other guys. Apparently Oscar entered Canada illegally. Oscar was a welder. He hired himself out to contractors who paid him cash. He lived in a basement suite with Miguel and four other guys from Guadalajara. Oscar got a welding job out of town. The job was north and east of Edmonton, near a lake. He'd worked for the guy a couple of times before. Miguel said that Oscar didn't like working for this guy, but the money was good. He called one of the men *de largo cabello plateado.*"

Lane waited for a translation.

"Long silver hair."

"What kind of welding was he doing?" Lane asked.

"Miguel didn't know. He just said that Oscar would make enough money so that he could go back to Guadalajara after he finished the job."

"No specific location?" Lane reached into his pocket and handed Nigel's gun back.

"Miguel kept saying that Oscar would talk about the bush." Nigel took the Glock in one hand and lifted his coffee cup with the other.

"We need a map." Lane downed the remains of his coffee and stood up.

"What for?" Nigel pushed his chair back.

"To see what's within a ten-hour radius of Calgary." Lane walked toward the Chev.

×

Chris Jones stood in line at a supermarket on the western edge of the city. He put a divider across the black conveyor belt and placed seven bags on the belt, each with its own twist tie. Each twist tie was wrapped precisely three times around the neck of each bag.

There were seven carrots, sticks of celery, tomatoes, cucumbers, potatoes, cobs of corn, and red peppers. He followed that with a box of oat bran cereal and two litres of milk. He put a divider behind his food and looked at the lady in front of him.

She was somewhere between sixty and seventy-five, weighed perhaps a pound over one hundred, and wore black leather, red high heels, and blonde hair.

"That's all?" the clerk asked.

The woman nodded at the clerk, then lifted her black leather purse, unzipped it, and reached inside for a black leather pocketbook. She unzipped one side of the pocketbook. Chris saw that the back of her left hand was a river system of purple veins dotted with liver-spot islands. The woman made a point of snapping each bill between her thumb and forefinger before handing it to the clerk.

Chris took a long, slow breath. He looked to his left and then down at the grey linoleum.

To his left and behind him stood a boy of two or three. Two blue eyes studied Chris from under a red baseball cap.

Chris looked back at the black-leather woman when she said, "Just a moment, I have the change." She closed one side of her pocketbook, turned it around, and unzipped the other side. She used a sapphire fingernail to dig into the change purse.

Chris breathed out slowly. Sweat rolled along his hairline. He felt a tug at the left knee of his jeans and looked down.

The toddler in the red cap was pointing his forefinger at Chris. The boy said something.

"What?" Chris asked.

"Booger!" The child went to wipe his forefinger on Chris's pants.

Chris stepped back. Panic gripped him just below the ribs. He backed into black-leather woman, who spilled her change over the counter and onto the floor.

"What is your problem?" She glared at him as she and the cashier began picking up the spilled coins. "Look what you've done!"

He looked again at the toddler, who was still hovering and focused on the green at the tip of his forefinger. Behind the child, the mother was reading a magazine as she leaned on a shopping cart and blocked Chris's other avenue of escape. He could feel his heart thumping, the air wheezing in and out of his lungs.

Chris turned, faced the counter, and leapt onto the conveyor belt. He glanced down at the clerk, who backed away open mouthed.

Chris tiptoed gingerly between vegetables and milk. He walked past the black-leather woman, reached the back edge of the counter, and leapt onto the floor. He turned in the direction of the exit, noting the stares of patrons and employees, and ran.

Lane's phone rang as he and Nigel spread a map of British Columbia, Alberta, and Saskatchewan over the conference room table.

Lane reached into his pocket and pulled out his phone. "Lane."

"Colin Weaver here. There has been a development."

He almost sounds excited. "I'm listening."

"The bullet fragment taken from the unknown victim —" Fibre said.

"— Oscar Mendes," Lane said.

Fibre hesitated for a moment. "The fragment taken from Mendes was a match to a bullet involved in a death near Lac La Biche, where a young woman was shot and killed as she rode in the passenger seat of a pickup truck. The shooter has yet to be identified and charged."

"Where did this happen, exactly?"

×

Donna lifted the mitre saw off the tailgate of her pickup and stepped onto the curb. She balanced on a ten-foot two-by-ten board as she walked over a freshly poured concrete driveway and into the garage. With practised efficiency, she set the saw atop its stand and clamped it in place. She went back outside to gather the rest of her tools.

Donna clipped on her tool belt and walked up to the front door where she had to balance on another two-by-ten board to keep her boots out of the mud. She hitched up the legs of her khaki overalls so she could stretch to reach the first step leading to the front door.

Inside, she checked the soles of her work boots and stepped into the front room with its twenty-foot ceiling and fireplace. The maple hardwood floors were covered with cardboard. She walked along the hallway and into the kitchen with its blue-tiled floor, maple cabinets, and blue-pearl marble coun-tertops. She looked around the kitchen at the pantry and the windows. *I'll start in here.*

Two hours later, her compressor filled the house with its clatter as she finished nailing the last section of trim around the kitchen windows.

She set her nail gun on the floor, turned, and measured for the next piece of trim along the floor.

"Ready for a break?"

Donna looked over her shoulder. Del Saunders stood in the middle of the kitchen with two cups of coffee.

"Perfect timing." She reached for a cup.

"Looks good, as always." Del stood on the other side of the kitchen in faded jeans and a tan work shirt. His blond hair was close cropped. His eyes took in the work she'd completed around windows and doors.

Donna took a sip of coffee and smiled.

"Where you been the last couple of weeks?" Del asked.

Donna looked past him at the kitchen cabinets, planning the angles and cuts she would need to make to frame them.

"Cut that out! You always do that when you don't want to answer a question. You let your mind wander back to the job," Del said.

Donna blushed and focused on him. "Getting ready for an anniversary."

"Lisa's?" Del asked.

Donna nodded.

"A big one?" Del asked.

"Very big." Donna nodded as she looked at the cup in her hand.

"There's something else I need to ask you about," Del said.

Donna watched his eyes as she sipped her coffee.

"I've got lots of work to do, and I've found a pair of finish-ing carpenters."

He's not making eye contact, Donna thought. "What's the catch?"

"They speak Spanish." Del noticed the disapproving tell around Donna's mouth and continued. "I've worked with them for a week. They're really good. Meticulous like you. You'd help me out if you would take them under your wing. Having two people working with you would really speed things up. I've got more work than I can handle, and I'd like to get things caught up again."

Donna shrugged.

"That means you'll think about it?"

"I'll think about it." Donna chewed her bottom lip. *Now is a good time to ask him. Sort of a favour for a favour.*

"Great! Thanks! I have to do an estimate on another job." Dell picked his phone out of his shirt pocket. "Christ, I'm late. Talk to you later." He turned and walked out of the kitchen.

She heard him move through the living room and shut the front door. *Shit. Why didn't you just ask him?*

Lane used his palms to flatten the map. "What did Fibre's e-mail say about the time of death?" he asked.

"About ten hours before the body was buried." Nigel stood across the table from Lane and studied the map.

Lane looked around the room. "We need to draw a circle of about one thousand kilometres around Calgary. I wonder if Lori has some string in her desk?" He looked through the glass to see Lori glaring at him over her computer screen.

"What did you do?" Nigel asked. "I've never seen her look at somebody that way before."

"Guess I'd better find out." Lane moved away from the table and stepped outside the conference room.

Lori held up a red folder. "You were supposed to pick

this up and read it. Then you were going to read the e-mail I sent you."

Lane could feel heat rising up from his neck to the tops of his ears. "I forgot."

"You're going to take this right now and read it as soon as you're finished with the map." She handed him the folder. Lori reached into her desk and handed him a roll of string. "What would you do without me?"

Lane tucked the folder under his arm and took the string. "I have no idea."

"Read what's in the folder. I'll send Nigel for coffee, and you sit down and read." Lori went back to typing.

I've been dismissed. Lane walked back into the conference room.

"What's that?" Nigel pointed at the folder.

"Some reading I have to do as soon as we draw a circle." Lane put the folder on the seat of a chair and began to measure the string using the scale at the bottom of the map. He took the length between the thumb and forefinger of his hands and put the left end on Calgary.

"Here, you'll need one of these." Lori poked her head into the room and tossed a pink highlighter to Nigel. "How do the two of you think you're going to find a killer using such high-tech tools?" She shut the door.

Lane looked at Nigel, who watched the thumb and forefinger of Lane's right hand as he made the circle.

"I don't think I've ever seen her this pissed off," Nigel said.

Neither have I. He stood back to look at the pink circle on the map. It encompassed parts of Saskatchewan, BC, the northern US, and most of Alberta.

"It's a huge area," Nigel said.

Lane nodded.

"Biche." Nigel pointed at a spot on the map. "Miguel kept saying *Biche.*"

Lane looked closely at Lac La Biche. He thought for a moment, turned to Nigel, and closed his eyes. *That was where the girl was shot.* Lane opened his eyes. "I want you to find out all you can about a thirteen-year-old unsolved shooting of a young woman near Lac La Biche."

"Now?" Nigel asked.

Lane glared at the young detective.

"Okay." Nigel left the conference room.

Lane looked at the red folder and sat down to read.

Half an hour later he reread the sections he'd highlighted from the police report.

Upon our arrival, the fifteen-year-old son (Nigel Li) opened the front door and discovered the body. He indicated that he had initiated the 911 call. He then led us to the kitchen where his mother was lying on the floor in front of the refrigerator. Her eyes were open, pupils fixed and dilated, and her blood was drying on the floor. The EMTs arrived approximately one minute later. Attempts at reviving the mother were unsuccessful.

I sat down with Nigel in the front room because the kitchen was becoming quite crowded. At that time he said, "My dad was mad at her because she said she was going to move out. They had a fight last night. The fight started up again when I was leaving for school this morning."

When I inquired about the location of his father, Nigel said, "Probably at work. He's obsessed with his job."

Lane flipped through the documents Lori had prepared for him. Another highlighted section from a social worker's report stared back at him.

Nigel Li has refused to be placed in the care of his uncle and aunt (Richard and Lucy Li). Nigel has proclaimed loudly and repeatedly that he will run away if placed with them. Nigel says, "My Uncle Richard and my father are cut from the same soiled cloth." Nigel insists that he will continue to live with a friend from school. Nigel has initiated a plan to move into a house near his school after the settlement of property issues related to the imprisonment of his father and death of his mother. In order to expedite the move, he retained the services of lawyer Thomas Pham.

Lane closed the file and looked through the glass wall of the conference room. He could see Nigel at his desk. The young man's brown eyes were focused intently on the computer screen.

Lane turned to look at Lori, who was watching him closely. She stood with her arms crossed as she leaned against the counter in front of her desk.

Lane thought, *How did I become a magnet for every stray human being living in this city?*

"Where's Matt?" Lane sat across from Arthur at the kitchen table. His meal consisted of pasta salad and half a chicken breast. *I'll lose weight for sure, but I don't know about Arthur. He could eat three romaine lettuce leaves a day and still gain weight.*

Arthur covered his mouth with the beefy fingers of his open right hand. "Sleeping." He chewed a bit more. "Again."

"Should I see whether he's hungry?" Lane asked.

Arthur set down his fork and turned his hands palms up over his plate. "It's up to you."

Lane studied Arthur's leaner, tanned face then asked, "What happened?"

Arthur considered the question before answering. "It's what isn't happening. No conversation. No going out. Work and sleep. He's turning into a hermit."

"And Christine and Dan?" Lane asked.

"They're out for dinner at his parents' place." Arthur rolled his eyes.

"What happened there?"

"We were invited." Arthur emphasized his point by aiming his fork at Lane.

"What does that mean?"

"Daniel's mother called about ten minutes ago to let us know we were invited, but her tone of voice said she was very relieved when I thanked her for the invitation and declined."

"Let the games begin?" Lane waited for some extra clue from his partner in order to figure out what exactly was going on with Christine and Matt.

"I don't know. Her reaction was odd. Very cheery. Very polite. Very relieved. The conversation had a weird edge to it. She was inviting us at the last minute, and I got the distinct impression that the entire process was calculated." He shrugged. "And just when I was getting used to having Dan around."

The door to Matt's downstairs bedroom opened, and they heard him walk across the hall to the bathroom.

Lane stood up and looked at Arthur. "I'll see if I can get him to join us." He walked downstairs to the family room. The TV was on, so he reached for the remote and shut it off.

Two minutes later, Matt opened the bathroom door and stood in the doorway in his black boxers.

"Join us for supper?" Lane saw his nephew look away.

Matt shook his head. There were dark circles under his eyes, and Lane could see Matt's ribs beneath the flesh.

"You need to eat something."

"No, I don't." Matt stepped into his bedroom and shut and locked the door.

Lane stared at the door, went to knock, changed his mind, and turned to go back upstairs.

×

"What the fuck do you two think you're doing?" Donna asked.

Lane looked right and saw Donna in overalls and a black T-shirt. Roz stopped and looked up at him. Lane took in the scene though the green lenses of his sunglasses. A pair of men stood at either end of a dresser mirror. Donna's voice had stopped them in the middle of the driveway of a two-storey house across the street from her place. A For Sale sign was stuck in the front lawn.

Donna said, "That's an antique, a family heirloom. Rhonda told me she was keeping that to give to her daughter. I've never seen you guys around here, and now you're walking out of Rhonda's house with an antique." She stood on the sidewalk across the street from Lane and within ten metres of the men with the mirror.

The taller man at the closer end of the mirror said, "Mind your own business, lady."

Lane heard the threat in the man's tone and checked for traffic before he began to cross the street. Roz followed behind.

Donna moved toward the front of the grey pickup truck backed up onto the driveway.

The man at the other end of the mirror wore a red-checked shirt. He spotted Lane, who turned to nod at the big man, but the man looked away.

"This *is* my business. I live in this neighbourhood. I live across the street, and you assholes are taking advantage of an old man who just lost his wife." Donna looked over her shoulder and spotted Lane.

Big man heaved his end of the antique onto the tailgate. "Listen, bitch, I told you to mind your own business." He made a step toward Donna.

Lane said, "At this point the real issue is whether it's theft under five thousand dollars or theft over." He caught a sweet whiff of alcohol on the breeze running down the street. Roz moved to his right and hit the end of her leash.

Big man hesitated and looked at Lane. "Who the hell are you?"

"Another neighbour." Lane pulled his phone out of his pocket.

The big man looked at Donna, who was standing at the other end of the pickup. He turned back to Lane. "What do you know about theft over?"

"It all depends on what the appraiser says about the value of an item. If it's theft over, then it's more serious than theft under five thousand dollars." Lane held his thumb over the face of the phone.

The man in the red-checked shirt set down his end of the mirror. "The old guy said we could have it."

"Then you won't mind if we ask him just to make sure there's no crime here." Lane pointed his phone at the big man.

Big Man and his red-checked partner looked at each other.

Donna said, "And we should get him to call his daughter, Linda. Her mother told me that bedroom set was promised to a member of the family." She turned to Lane. "Rhonda died six months ago, and the house went up for sale just last week. Her daughter Linda found a place for her father in Arbour Lake. He's in the early stages of dementia."

Lane looked at the big man, who was lifting the mirror off the pickup's tailgate.

"Until we can verify everyone's story, how about the two of you gently set the mirror down in the garage?" Lane moved closer as the second man set his end of the mirror on the grass, let go, and moved to the passenger door of the truck.

The big man made his move toward the pickup as Lane grabbed for the mirror. He managed to reach it before it could smash against the concrete.

Donna grabbed the other end.

Two truck doors slammed. The truck started. Big Man shifted into gear, the engine roared, the tires chirped, and Red-Checked Shirt stuck up his middle finger. It remained framed in the middle of the rear window as the truck sped through the playground zone. On the trailer hitch, a pair of silver balls rocked back and forth.

"Assholes," Donna said.

Lane pressed a button on his phone and held it to his ear. "Detective Lane. UHG 222. Will exit either at Nose Hill Drive and Ranchlands Boulevard or Ranchlands and John Laurie. Suspected impaired driver. Ask traffic to follow and stop for any and all infractions." Lane pressed another button and put the phone in his pocket. "Let me tie Roz to the railing, and we can move this back into the garage."

Roz whimpered and tugged against the leash as they hefted the mirror inside the garage and leaned it against an inside wall.

"How come you did that?" Donna gave her hands a swipe down the front of her coveralls.

"Did what?" Lane followed her out of the garage and into the sun.

"Got involved. You could have just walked past." Donna went up the front steps and knocked on the door.

"It looked wrong, and I've walked by your house a few times. You always say hello. Those two guys looked out of place. It wasn't because I thought you needed help." Lane smiled.

The door opened and a man with a full head of white hair and vacant eyes asked, "Lisa?"

"Lisa was my sister," Donna said.

"Oh." The old man looked confused.

"Who were the guys taking the mirror?" Donna pointed at the antique.

"They said they were furniture movers," the old man said.

"I'm gonna call your daughter. Can you close the garage door until she gets here?" Donna backed down the steps.

Lane and Donna waited until the garage door closed.

"Alzheimer's?" Lane ventured.

"Looks like it. Rhonda was able to handle him on her own, but then she got sick and died. Now he's lost," Donna said. "Got time for a beer?"

Lane thought, *I should go home but Arthur has turned into a cancer victim and Matt, well, he's* . . . "I'd love a beer." He untied Roz and followed Donna across the street.

He spotted her pickup parked on the street in front of a white van. The words *Beauty could use a little help to save the world* were painted in pink along both side panels.

She led him to the back of her two-storey house. The yard was tidy, and two chairs sat on either side of a glass-topped table on a red-brick patio bordered by blue flowers. "Have a seat," Donna invited.

Lane sat down, and Roz lay down on the grass with a harrumph. "Don't worry, you'll get your walk."

Donna returned with two long-necked bottles and two glasses. She poured one beer and handed it to Lane, then poured one for herself and raised her glass. "Thanks for the help. It was lucky you came along."

Lane shrugged. "It's my neighbourhood, too." He took a sip of the beer and caught the sweet, subtle taste of honey. He looked through the glass at its amber colour. "This is very good. Where did you get it?"

"Made it."

Lane took another sip and looked past her through the

open kitchen door. On the wall was a picture of a woman wearing desert camouflage. "You were in the forces?" he asked.

"No, but my twin sister was a medic in Afghanistan."

Was? Lane thought. *From the tone of her voice, she doesn't want to talk about it.* "What kind of work do you do?"

Donna used her left hand to rub Roz behind the ears. The dog closed her eyes and crawled closer to Donna. "I'm a finishing carpenter."

Lane nodded.

"It's my own company. Started up a few years ago, and I've been busy ever since." She smiled. "I found out I like working for myself. How about you?"

This is where the conversation usually gets interesting. "I'm a homicide detective with the Calgary Police Service." He watched her hand and saw it hesitate for a moment before she went back to rubbing Roz's ear.

"So that's why you knew how to handle those two thieves with the pickup truck." She took another sip of beer.

"Years of practice at learning how to read people." He lifted his glass and tipped it toward Donna.

Donna raised her glass and tilted it toward Lane. "Years of practice at learning how to think of all the angles before starting a job."

$$\times$$

Arthur was watching TV when Lane got home. Lately, Arthur stayed up until two or three in the morning. Then he would sleep in until ten or eleven. The pattern had emerged over the winter and now appeared to be his routine.

Lane went to bed. He thought the clatter of an aluminum ladder woke him up around one o'clock.

chapter 4

Suspected Bomb Plotters Arrested

In a joint operation, the RCMP and CSIS have arrested five people suspected of plotting to bomb targets in the Greater Toronto Area.

Four men and one woman were detained in a series of coordinated arrests late Friday afternoon in and around the GTA.

Sixty circuit boards for detonating explosive devices were seized at the same time.

Police have not yet released the names of the suspects. Police spokesperson Staff Sergeant Roly Greene says the suspects may be part of a larger organization.

Story continues page A7

Lane's phone rang. He gripped the newspaper in his left hand and picked up the phone. "Mornin'."

"It's Harper."

Lane leaned forward when he heard the no-nonsense tone in his friend's voice. He set the paper down. "What's up?"

"It appears we have a problem. We received a complaint from the manager of Foothills Fertilizers. This morning he reported that approximately fifty litres of nitric acid are missing. We also have the recent theft of fifty litres of sulphuric acid from a chrome shop. Two pharmacies in the northwest have reported unusually large sales of glycerine. As you know from Keely, this combination of ingredients is a red flag. She's on her way to Calgary."

"Do you want me to pick her up at the airport?" Lane asked.

"No. I want you and Li to make this Foothills Fertilizers investigation priority number one. I know it's not your normal type of work, but I want you on it. There are indications we're working against the clock on this one."

Lane waited when he sensed Harper had more to say.

"John A. Jones has dropped out of sight. The local RCMP detachment stopped by for a visit, and no one was on site. We don't yet know whether any of these events are connected. My hope is that you will tell me they aren't, and then we don't have a problem."

Lane said, "I'll pick up Nigel and head out to Foothills Fertilizers to see whether we can get a lead on the missing chemicals."

"Keep me informed of your progress." Harper hung up.

Chris Jones used an ohmmeter to check the connections on the refrigeration unit. He turned the meter off, wrapped up the wires, set it down, and plugged the compressor in.

The unit wheezed, thumped, then settled into a comfortable rhythm.

He turned to the open laptop he'd set up on the bench against the wall. He pointed the cursor at fifty litres of sulphuric acid listed on the open file. "Just make sure it's all here."

Chris hitched his green camouflage pants and turned to the adjacent wall where a matched pair of twenty-five–litre stainless-steel containers sat on their wooden bases.

He turned back to the computer and checked the next item on the list. Fifty litres of nitric acid was stored against the opposite wall.

Chris crouched. His knees cracked. He counted the cases of glycerine stacked beneath the bench. He stood up, saw a snowstorm of stars in front of his eyes, then steadied himself with his hands braced on the bench until the head spins eased. His vision cleared, and he checked the digits entered in the laptop. Then he repeated the counting process four more times.

When he was done counting, Chris pulled on goggles, a helmet, and a pair of elbow-length PVC gloves. "Should have it all prepared by the end of the day."

×

Nigel stood on the sidewalk outside of his trendy brick-fronted two-storey infill. It was situated on a hill where mature trees stretched their limbs to touch the leaves of trees on the other side of the street in front of his house. The LRT whispered its way along the crest of the hill two blocks north of Nigel's home. Below Nigel's house was the neighbourhood of Hill-hurst, where wartime houses were gradually being replaced with new homes.

Lane pulled up to the curb.

Nigel climbed in the passenger side. "What's up?"

"We have to check out some missing nitric acid." Then Lane thought, *Nigel's having trouble doing up his seat belt.*

"What about Oscar's killer?" Nigel locked his seat belt in place and groaned.

Lane headed down the hill and figured out the best way to get back onto Crowchild Trail. "Harper made this our main priority. Along with the missing nitric acid, sulphuric acid has been stolen, and sales of glycerine have spiked in the northwest."

Nigel nodded as Lane pulled up to a red light and stopped behind a black compact. "Look at that." He pointed and laughed.

"What?" Lane looked right and left.

"The bumper sticker on the car ahead of us."

Lane looked at the rear of the black car.

"It says 'NICE TRUCK' and then in smaller print, 'Too bad about the tiny penis.'" Nigel looked to his right and spotted a Tim Hortons. "Want a cup of coffee?"

I can read. No, we don't have time for a cup of coffee right now, Lane thought, then demurred: *Take it easy on the kid. If I don't, Lori will take it out on my hide.* "What happened to your ribs?"

Nigel rubbed his left side at the memory. "I was boxing last night. This guy kept hitting me with his right. Feels like I've been tenderized."

The light turned green. Lane followed the black car onto Crowchild and travelled south.

"Where is Foothills Fertilizers?" Nigel asked.

"Way south. How come you're not asking why we're tracking down chemicals instead of Oscar's killer?"

"It's kind of obvious. I mean, no offence, but those three chemicals make nitro, it's Stampede week, and there are always a few crazies around who want to make some kind of statement. We don't need an Oklahoma or a Twin Towers happening in this city." Nigel looked down at the river as they drove over the bridge.

Now. Ask him now. "When were you going to tell me about your Uncle Tran connection?"

Nigel blushed and turned to face his partner. "I phoned him when I found out I'd be working with you. I asked him what I should do. He gave me one of those maddening bits of advice he always gives. He said the decision was mine to make and that you are a detective who will figure things out. That you will ask me if you want to know the answer. You know what he's like. He's a wise man who thinks I need to find my own way. And he gives me nothing but ambiguous clues that leave me wondering what exactly I'm supposed to do."

Lane nodded. "I know what he's like." *And it turns out he's right.*

"I owe him a lot." Nigel looked out the window as they climbed out of the river valley. "After my mom died, one of my friends at school put me in touch with Uncle Tran. Then Tran got me a lawyer. At that point, things began to turn around for me. Up to that point, I was just a victim."

"He's an unusual man."

"The really unusual thing is that the family — Uncle Tran's family — well, they think they owe you. And when one owes you, they all owe you. Do you have any idea how big Uncle Tran's family is?" Nigel asked as they passed under an overpass.

"I don't know, fifty people?" Lane pulled into the left lane.

Nigel laughed and stuck his thumb in the air. "Fifteen hundred."

Lane looked at his partner and was greeted by a smug smile.

"You're kidding, right?" Lane asked.

Nigel shook his head. "Not at all. We had a family reunion in June. One thousand five hundred and two people showed up."

"Where was the reunion?" Lane asked.

"Out on an acreage west of town. It was the only venue big enough for all of us."

"Where do you keep your lucky elephant?"

Nigel patted his chest. "Right here."

"I don't get it," Lane said.

"You don't get what?"

Lane eased into the centre lane and then into the right lane so they could make the overpass and join Glenmore Trail. "I don't get why they said you're a pain in the ass." Lane eased off the throttle and coasted uphill to bleed off some speed. He smiled. "Well, I mean, you are a pain in the ass, but not a total pain."

Nigel smiled back. "No, I was a real pain in the ass to those other cops."

"How come?" Lane eased left as the overpass turned east.

"They wouldn't listen to me. Just like . . ." Nigel said.

"Just like?"

"Just like the detective who wouldn't listen to me when I told him that my father killed my mother." Nigel looked south across the Glenmore Reservoir where sails dotted the surface. "I tried to tell him that my dad was a control freak, and my mom was going to leave him. I tried to tell him that my dad would be at work carrying on as if nothing had happened. That my dad would have a plausible story to tell them when they went to question him. The detective treated me like a kid who knew nothing and could tell him nothing. He turned out to be just like those other cops I was paired with. So, when they wouldn't listen, I wouldn't shut up."

Lane looked ahead, did a shoulder check, and changed lanes. *Some cops can be like that, but that doesn't mean being a jerk in response will work.*

"How come you do? Listen, I mean."

Lane thought for a moment, then said, "If you listen to what people say and listen to the way they say it—especially if you listen to their tone of voice—you can learn a whole bunch about people, who they are, and what they're really up to. And usually, it's way more than the person wishes to reveal."

Nigel started to reply, then closed his mouth and sat quietly for the rest of the trip.

Glenmore Trail eased down under Elbow Drive as Lane continued east, crossed the river again, and travelled into Ogden's industrial area. They pulled up in front of Foothills Fertilizers, a rectangular white two-storey building with a grey BMW parked out front. A man in a burgundy golf shirt and khaki dress pants looked up from the face of his cell phone and frowned. His hair was black and so was his mood.

"He's late for a tee time, and he's pissed." Lane opened his door and climbed out. He heard Nigel groan as he got out of the car.

"I'm Steven Davies. I've been waiting for sixty-five minutes. I hope I haven't inconvenienced you." He fingered his goatee.

Lane reached for his ID. "Mr. Davies, I'm Detective Lane and this is Detective Li. You have some missing nitric acid. Please show us where the chemical is stored." He walked past Davies and toward the door. Lane opened it before Davies could react. Davies was forced to run to catch up with Lane.

"It's this way." Davies pointed as he ran ahead of Lane and opened a door marked EMPLOYEES ONLY.

The storage area was air conditioned, and the hazardous material containers sat in rows on low shelves. Davies pointed at the largest silver stainless-steel container in the room. "At least fifty litres of nitric acid are missing."

Nigel reached for his cell phone and used his thumbs to take notes.

Lane took a look at the other containers. "You store sulphuric acid as well?"

Davies shook his head. "No. We use only nitric acid here. I do spot checks every so often."

"How long ago was the last spot check?" Lane asked.

"One month to the day," Davies said.

"We're going to need a list of employees and their contact information," Lane said.

Davies rolled his eyes. "Right at this moment?"

Lane took a step closer to Davies and caught an offensively potent whiff of aftershave. "I'm afraid so. We appreciate your diligence. You must be aware that nitric acid, in combination with other chemicals, is used in the manufacture of an explosive?"

"Of course." Davies looked at his watch. "That's why I keep a close eye on it."

Not close enough, apparently. And he wears a Rolex. This guy is a walking cliché. "I'm afraid we will have to inconvenience you further. Our Forensic Crime Scene Unit is on its way to gather evidence from the storage room."

"Any idiot knows that the person who took the acid would have been wearing PVC gloves! You won't get fingerprints off any of the containers," Davies said.

Nigel began to chuckle.

Lane stopped him with a glance. "It's what's inside the PVC gloves that interests us." His phone rang. He pulled it from his pocket and turned his back on Davies. "Hello."

"It's Harper. We need you downtown as soon as possible."

"On our way." Lane pressed the end button and pointed his phone at Davies. "You, or another representative of your company, will remain here until the forensic unit completes its work."

"I have an appointment." Davies crossed his arms as if to indicate that he was in control of this situation.

"I'm afraid you'll have to cancel the golf." Lane turned and left.

✕

Donna had just finished the first floor of another new house and was heading home. She drove east along John Laurie Boulevard. The summer sun filled the cab with the scents of oak and maple sawdust. Each time she crested a hill, the grey tips of the Rocky Mountains set their teeth into the horizon. Then she spotted the Eagle's Nest sign. About fifty people surrounded the sign, looking up at the words on the white background.

Donna leaned forward and squinted through the windshield to read the words.

DON'T JUST SAY YOU BELIEVE IN GOD KNOW HIM IN MOHAMMED

She passed the gathering and heard the angry chatter through her open window. Donna turned left at the next set of lights and wound her way home. She pulled into her driveway and shut off the engine. She used her fingers to count off the days until Friday. "Six days to go."

✕

Keely sat in a conference room across the table from Harper and Chief Simpson. Lane saw that she'd let her unruly red hair grow longer so that it fell onto her shoulders, and although she looked tired, she seemed to be thriving. "Good to see you," Lane said.

Keely smiled, got up, and hugged him. "How's everyone?"

Lane smiled. "Just fine."

Keely stepped back, cocked her head to one side, and studied him. "Are you lying to me?"

Lane ignored the question and turned to his new partner. "This is Nigel Li."

Keely shook Nigel's hand. "I hope you realize how lucky you are to be partnered with Lane."

"People keep telling me that." Nigel paused before he added, "People I respect."

"We need to get down to it. Keely has been sent to us as a liaison between the RCMP and CSIS." Harper waited for them to sit. "Keely, get us started."

Keely opened the file in front of her and picked up an eight-by-ten photograph. "This is John A. Jones." She handed it to Harper, who passed it to Lane and Nigel.

The man in the photo appeared to be at least fifty, with shoulder-length white hair and intense blue eyes that stared directly into the camera.

Keely said, "We suspect he's been behind several pipeline bombings near Lac La Biche. The local RCMP detachment tried to find him earlier in the week. Jones has dropped out of sight."

Lane looked at the photo, trying to think why it was tickling his memory.

Nigel said, "A source named Miguel said that Oscar Mendes worked for a man with long silver hair. We believe Oscar was working somewhere near Lac La Biche."

Keely turned to Lane, who said, "We have nothing solid to go on, but our investigation was leading us to Jones's stomping grounds. The witness was close to Oscar Mendes and provided us with the information."

"Who is this Oscar Mendes exactly?" Keely asked.

"He was shot in the back, and his body dumped in the basement of a new home. A bullet fragment from his body was matched to the unsolved shooting of a young woman near Lac La Biche," Lane said.

Harper gestured for Jones's photograph. "So we have missing nitric acid, stolen sulphuric acid, higher than usual sales of glycerine, a new killing that seems to be connected to an old one, and a religious zealot we're unable to locate. Is that all that we've got so far?"

"That's not all of it, actually." Nigel nodded in Lane's direction. "I was asked to research the unsolved murder of the young woman. Jones told investigators that he did not want to know who shot the girl, but she was trespassing on his property. Jones now appears to be in a deteriorating state of denial. His wife died of breast cancer last month. Two women from his community — or cult — left with their children a week after the funeral. They said they questioned Jones's leadership. That his behaviour was becoming erratic, that he threatened them and their children. They ended up in Edmonton in a women's shelter. The reports are here." Nigel tapped a red folder and took a breath. "Jones is also a member of a Christian Aryan Nations group."

Lane glanced around the table. Keely met his gaze. Harper's face was red. Simpson was listening and frowning. Lane thought, *Nigel, do you have to sound so damned condescending?*

Nigel continued, apparently unaware of his effect on the others around the table. "Since the death of his wife and the departure of the two women — one of them, by the way, was his daughter — there has been a power struggle within the community. One of the men in the community apparently asked some questions of Jones and was excommunicated. So there's been a fracturing of the community, resulting in a tremendous upheaval in John A. Jones's control over his life and those he led. Two weeks ago he spoke to a CBC reporter. Jones blamed fracking for his wife's cancer. He holds several oil companies responsible for her death. One of his most pointed comments was, 'People in the city will never understand the way that oil companies are poisoning people in the rural areas until it happens to them.' That comment was made one week ago." Nigel pointed at his laptop. "I can play the clip for you." He looked around the table. Nigel saw that Harper was watching Lane. Keely was in the process of closing her mouth.

Lane thought, *Remember how important it is to listen to this guy. It all comes out like the voice of a commentator, implying we're all imbeciles if we don't see things the way he does. Still, Nigel may have a point.* "You've given us lots of information. What conclusions have you reached?"

Nigel dropped his eyes to stare at the red folder. "Men like John A. Jones need to feel they're in control. Jones lost his wife and has also lost control of at least some of the people he thought were his followers. His generalized threat to people who live in cities, combined with his disappearance and allegations that connect him with bombing of installations near various oil and gas facilities, leads me to believe that he is planning a major act of violence and targeting a major urban centre."

"Do you have any concrete proof of a link between Jones and this city?" Harper used a deliberate monotone.

"No." Nigel's face reddened. "But I'm right. I know I'm right."

Lane put his hand on Nigel's forearm.

Harper shook his head and took a long breath. "All right."

"You guys done?" Keely asked.

Harper frowned at Nigel, who gritted his teeth.

"Good. I'm tired of being the only woman in the room when there's a pissing contest going on. It's the same game they play in Ottawa." Keely tapped her laptop. "The fact is that John A. Jones was recorded making a call to a Calgary number. It's a business called Foothills Fertilizers."

Lane and Nigel looked at one another.

Harper took a look at Simpson, who leaned in closer as he focused on Keely.

Lane said, "We haven't figured out who Jones's connection is yet. What time was the call made?"

Keely scrolled down the page. "Ten o'clock, Thursday night."

Nigel asked, "How did you connect those five conspirators to the plans for attacks in the GTA?"

Keely leaned back, looked at Nigel, frowned, and stared at Nigel. "How did you know that?"

Nigel turned his palms up. "It was a reasonable deduction."

"We use a variety of techniques and are reluctant to share them," Keely said.

"So this information sharing goes one way only?" Nigel held his right hand out, palm up.

Enough of this! Lane stood up and smiled. "You said we have only a week. We have to track down Jones. Our first step is to find out who was on the cleaning crew at Foothills Fertilizers on Thursday night. Then we'll have a short list of suspects."

"And who wants to bet that one of them has given false contact information?" Nigel asked.

"Do you always have to have the last word?" Harper asked.

"Yes." Nigel turned to face Harper. "So, does this mean we're still on the Oscar Mendes case?"

"We've got some work to do." Lane took Nigel by the arm and led him out of the conference room.

✕

Chris Jones pulled the PVC glove from his left hand, took the face shield off, and carefully set the equipment down on the workbench a metre away from the laptop.

He looked inside a pair of white refrigerators. Each had

its shelves removed to accommodate a seventy-five–litre stainless-steel container on the bottom. Each container held the mixture of nitric acid, sulphuric acid, and glycerine. He checked the thermometer in the first fridge, gently closed the door, and repeated the procedure at the second fridge. He ran his fingers around the magnetic seals to insure that each fridge door was properly closed.

Chris moved over to the laptop and entered the date, time, and temperature. He went to the door of the garage, opened it, and squinted at the sunshine.

×

Lane's phone rang as he held the office door open for Nigel. Lane fumbled in his pocket for the phone and looked at caller ID. "Harper?"

"Are you alone?" Harper asked.

"Yep." Lane stayed outside of the office and let the door close while Nigel went inside, sat at his desk, and began working on his computer.

"It was a mistake to partner you with Nigel," Harper said.

"What?" *The kid really did get on your nerves, Cam.*

"I mean we thought that if anyone could work with Nigel, you could, but he's impossible. I knew he was a problem, but that's an understatement. He's an arrogant pain in the ass. If we weren't in the middle of this Jones case, I would pull him right now."

And Nigel may well be right about Jones. "I'll let you know if it was a mistake."

"Okay, but don't feel like you have to make it work. He's an arrogant little prick." Harper hung up.

Lane walked into the office, sat down, and leaned back in his chair. He looked at the ceiling. *Yes, he's difficult, but his assessment of Jones is probably sound. And he does need to learn the difference between confidence and arrogance.*

He turned to Nigel. "We need to find out who was working at Foothills Fertilizers on Thursday night. Who has their cleaning contract?"

"I'll find out," Nigel said.

Lane's phone rang. "Lane."

"There are reports that John A. Jones was spotted in Edmonton this morning," Keely said.

"You think he's headed this way?"

"My sources say that his community has fractured and he may have been forced out. So, if Nigel is correct, we may have a messianic zealot with access to explosives and nothing to lose."

"Thanks. I think." Lane ended the connection.

An hour later, Nigel set down his phone and looked away from his computer. "Of the three employees working Thursday night at Foothills, one doesn't check out. The phone number he gave is out of service. The address is for a house in Sunnyside that's been demolished."

"Sunnyside is just across the river from where Oscar Mendes was buried," Lane said.

Nigel nodded. "The guy gave his name as Chris Wright. A Chris Wright with the same birthday died twenty years ago, one week after being born in Fort McMurray."

"Any photographs?" Lane asked.

"Yes." Nigel pointed at the screen.

Lane got up and looked at the image of a nondescript, round-faced young man smiling at the camera. "Looks like he could pass unnoticed almost anywhere."

Lane went back to reading the autopsy report on Oscar Mendes.

They took an hour for lunch on Stephen Avenue. The mall was awash with jeans, cowboy hats, western shirts, boots, and the twang of country and western bands making a few extra dollars working for the Stampede. A woman with blonde hair, tight jeans, Botoxed lips, and generous cleavage was covering Patsy Cline's "Crazy." She was backed up by a man on bass who wore an ancient white Stetson, a curly-waxed moustache, and a beer belly hanging over the top half of his belt buckle. The woman on drums was half the age of the other two and wore a ball cap to cover her turquoise hair. *She can actually play,* Lane thought.

A little further down, four square-dancing couples followed the orders of a caller in a black Stetson who told them to allemande left. Lane caught a glimpse of frilled pink panties under white crinoline.

Lane held the door to The Diner and let Nigel go in first.

"Never been here before," Nigel said.

The sounds of voices, dishes, and an espresso machine were complemented by the scents of coffee, chocolate, fresh fruit, and bacon.

Nigel looked at the row of red tractor chairs along the counter. "Never seen a place like this before."

"For two?" a dark-haired woman asked. The sleeves of her black blouse were rolled up, revealing scars running horizontally and vertically up her forearm.

Lane nodded. She led them past the crowded counter and up the stairs to a table near the kitchen.

"Coffee?" the woman asked.

Lane turned his coffee cup right side up and smiled. Nigel did the same.

Lane added raw sugar and cream. A waitress arrived with a carafe of coffee, put down two menus, filled their cups, and moved to the next table. Lane put down his spoon, lifted the cup, and closed his eyes as he sipped.

Nigel drank his with double the sugar.

There was a lull in the conversations around them. Lane looked at the stone walls next to his elbow. "Go easy on Harper. He was my partner. He's a good man."

Nigel opened his mouth.

Lane held up a finger and cocked his head to one side. "He has our backs. We should give him the same courtesy, don't you think?"

Nigel put his coffee down. "If you say so."

Lane nodded. *You don't sound convinced, but I do say so.* "Can we lose the sarcasm? We're partners. Got any plans for the Stampede?"

Nigel stared back at his partner for a moment then smiled, nodded, and inhaled. "I'll try. Stampede's not my style. How about you?"

"I like the fireworks, but that's about it."

After lunch, they returned to their work. Nigel spoke again at five o'clock. "I think I've got something."

Lane got up and looked at Nigel's computer screen. Nigel pointed at an image of Chris Wright on the left side of the screen. Then he pointed to a group shot of men, women, and children sitting on wooden steps. Behind them, John A. Jones stood on the top step under the gable of a two-storey log house. Nigel enlarged the image and pointed at a young man of eighteen or nineteen who stood next to John A. "Looks like the same person as the missing guy from Foothills Fertilizers."

Yes, it does. "Name?"

"Chris Jones," Nigel said.

And you didn't say 'I told you so.' Maybe there is hope for you. Lane patted Nigel on the shoulder.

×

It was dark by the time Lane decided to take Roz for a walk. Matt was asleep, Arthur was snoring on the couch, and Christine and Dan were at a movie. *There's a connection between Mendes and Jones, I'm sure of it,* Lane thought.

The sky was clear, and the stars were winking. Mars was especially bright in the sky. Lane felt himself beginning to relax as the rhythm of walking allowed him to make sense of the last three days. Roz trotted alongside, every so often looking up at him for reassurance.

They walked past Donna's house. Again he read the words painted along the side of the van: *Beauty could use a little help to save the world.*

They walked until they reached Nose Hill Drive; then they turned and walked home. It was a rare night when light clothing was comfortable after dark.

They were close to home when they reached the elementary school across from the strip mall. Lane crossed the street, climbed up to the level of the strip mall's parking lot, and sat down on the curb. Roz sat next to him with her rear legs tucked to one side. Behind them were the windows of the International Kickboxing School. Beside that was the Islamic Centre.

Roz bristled and began to growl. A coyote with a ragged tail walked down the middle of the street and turned into the school parking lot.

Lane looked left down the parking lot and saw an SUV with two silhouettes sitting in the front watching him.

He looked right and saw a pickup truck with two more shadows turned his way.

The heads inside the truck turned to look past him.

The farting rumble of an exhaust spoiled the quiet. Lane looked left. A low-slung vehicle hid behind its headlights and eased over a speed bump.

The engine revved. The body scraped over the bump. The car moved closer.

Lane saw the windows on the passenger side open up. A barrel stuck out the front window. Another poked out of the window behind. Lane looked for cover and saw there was none. He leaned forward onto his feet, crouched, and heard his knees pop.

Lane heard the whine of an engine's starter.

The low-slung car pulled in front of the Islamic Centre and the barrels of the guns began to spit. Paintballs slapped against the glass of the Islamic Center.

The car's engine screamed and so did its tires.

The truck to Lane's right pulled ahead to block the exit.

The car squealed to a stop. Its horn blared.

The SUV pulled up behind the car, filled its cabin with light, and tapped its rear bumper. Then the parking lot and shop glass flashed with reflected rotating white, red, and blue light.

Lane heard doors opening.

"On the ground!" The order came from behind the wall of lights from the SUV.

The passenger door of the car flew open. The face of a sixteen-year-old boy was illuminated, his eyes wide and white. He ran to the sidewalk and sprinted toward Lane. Lane stood up, leaned left, stuck out an elbow, and the boy careened into the glass of the International Kickboxing School. He skidded face first onto the sidewalk. Lane sat on his back.

"Asshole!" the boy said.

Roz barked and growled. Lane held her by the collar.

"Fucking asshole!" the boy shouted.

Lane watched as the driver and the other passenger of the car got out to lay face down on the pavement in the glare of their headlights.

"Get the fuck off me!" the boy screamed.

A voice from behind the headlights of the pickup said, "You!"

Lane blinked at the glare and pointed at his chest. "Me?"

"Yes, you!" the officer said.

"Get him the fuck off of me!" the boy whined.

"What?" Lane put his hands in the air. *I'm trying to help you out here. Now I understand why Nigel enjoys being such a pain.*

"Who the hell are you?" the officer asked.

"Who the hell are you?" Lane asked.

"My mom's a fuckin' MLA. She's Laura Poulin! So you'd better get off of me!" the boy said.

Lane laughed. "Of course she is."

The officer said, "I'm Corporal Lesley."

Lane heard the arrogance behind the voice. "I'm Detective Lane."

There was quiet for a moment. Then the officers moved out from behind the headlights.

Lane looked to his left and saw the officers placing handcuffs on the wrists of the boys, who lay on their bellies in front of their car.

Unnecessarily, Lesley shone a flashlight in Lane's eyes, then in Mr. Poulin's face.

Lesley looked over his shoulder at the officers cuffing the other two suspects. "It is Lane." He tapped Lane on the shoulder. "It's okay. I've got this son of an MLA."

Lesley's voice has lost its edge.

Lesley said, "Thanks for the help, Lane."

Lane heard his name used in a different tone now, a respectful tone. It happened more often since Chief Smoke resigned. Lane had even heard the words *smoke* and *joke* in the same sentence. "It might be best to have this scene taped off and ask forensics to gather evidence."

Lesley lifted Poulin to his feet, nodded at Lane, and turned to the other officers. "Tape it off!"

chapter 5

Record Crowds Attend Stampede

If you think it's crowded at the fairground this weekend, you're right, and Tourism Calgary is smiling.

Rene Amour, spokesperson for Tourism Calgary, says, "Hotels and motels are filled to capacity. Restaurants and bars are experiencing lineups."

Record numbers of visitors have been arriving at the gates of the Stampede Grounds in the early days of this year's crowd-pleasing events.

Rob Spence, a member of the Stampede board, smiles from under his black Stetson. "If the weather holds, we're hoping to break a few attendance records this year."

"Do you do shit like this just to aggravate me?" Harper asked.

"Like what?" Lane sat in a chair on his deck with an empty cup of coffee, the Sunday paper, and his cell phone. Roz was next to him, her chin resting on her paws.

"Like arresting MLA Laura Poulin's son. The same Laura Poulin who's always so happy to tell us she's a third-generation Albertan who stands up for the values that make this province prosperous. The same Laura Poulin who says she's proud to back the blue," Harper said.

"Oh, baaaby, I'm prairie doggin' it for you!"

"What the hell is that?" Harper asked.

"There's a Stampede breakfast down at the community centre. A country and western band is playing —" Lane glanced at a newspaper headline predicting record crowds at the grandstand "— badly. They've got speakers pounding out this stuff."

"Baaaby, I'm turtle headin' it for you!"

"My gawd that's awful," Harper said.

"Tell me about it. Reminds me of Ms. Poulin: no tact, no rhythm, no brain, and lots of noise." Lane plugged his left ear with his index finger, muffling the words to the music.

"I phoned to thank you for suggesting that Officer Lesley request forensics at the scene. Young Poulin's prints were all over one of the paintball guns. He tried to deny that he was in the car. Then he blamed the two other boys. Now we have three sets of parents all blaming one another and, you understand, no direct calls from Ms. Poulin's office but quite a few calls from concerned citizens voicing their displeasure with the police service. And they are all very aware of even the most inconsequential details of the arrest. Then there are those who support what the boys did. One caller said, 'The boys were just acting on what everyone is saying about those people and their religion anyway.' I'm hoping this mess will all die down soon."

"Last night, the officers were waiting to block off both exits. How did you know the drive-by was going to happen?" Lane asked.

"Keely," Harper said.

"How?"

"Communications."

Lane waited.

"That's all she would say when I asked. Now you know as much as I do," Harper said.

"You mean it's all very hush-hush RCMP Official Secrets Act?"

"Very. Any more progress with Jones?" Harper asked.

"Nigel identified Chris Jones as one of the Foothills employees who worked Thursday night. Indications are that it was John A. Jones's son who took the nitric acid."

"Shit. That's all we need with everything else that's going on, a religious zealot with a bomb."

Lane waited.

"I'll pass it on to Keely. You keep at it."

Lane took his phone away from one ear and his finger from the other.

"Baby, I'm overloaded with love for you!" The rest of the song was cut mercifully short when Lane followed Roz inside and shut the door behind them.

✕

Chris Jones wore desert camouflage pants and a long-sleeved khaki shirt. He stepped into the garage where his nose caught a hint of the chemicals he'd mixed the day before.

He opened his laptop and tapped the EXTRACTION PLANT file. He looked at his watch and entered the time.

Then he moved to the first fridge and used his left hand to steady it while he eased the door open with his right. The light inside blinked on.

The thermometer set on the shelf inside the door read eight degrees Celsius. Chris eased the door closed until he could feel the magnetic seal engage across the tips of his fingers. He moved to the next fridge and repeated the process.

Then he went to the laptop and entered the temperatures.

×

Arthur and Matt stared blankly at the TV mounted on the wall of the downstairs family room. Light shone in through the south-facing doors. The shadow of the neighbours' evergreen was creeping in from the right side of the glass. The rerun reality show pitted a group of young men and women against one another on a set that reminded Lane of a prison, because the people couldn't leave until someone else told them to. He looked at Matt, whose eyes were half closed as he reclined in the armchair. Across from him, Arthur lay on the couch with his head propped up by an oversized pillow. *The two of you are beginning to look and act like zombies.* Lane got up and went upstairs, filled the kettle, turned it on, and ground up some coffee beans.

The phone rang. He reached for it and recognized the number. "Good morning, Keely."

"Have you had your coffee yet?"

"Just in the process of making a second cup."

"I've got some news on Jones."

"Which one?" He tapped the ground beans into the Bodum.

"The older one has been visiting cash machines in Fort McMurray and Edmonton. By the latest tally he has twenty-five hundred cash in his pocket. It's a smart move, I think. He's getting ready to hit the road and doesn't want us tracking him with his plastic."

Another indication he may be heading our way. "When

did he make his last withdrawal?" He poured boiling water into the Bodum.

"About nine o'clock last night in Edmonton." Keely took a breath, then asked, "Any luck tracking down the son?"

"Not yet. Fake address, phone not in service. We have to assume he's somewhere in the northwest because of the glycerine purchases, but that's all we've got besides the picture." Lane set the timer on the microwave for four minutes.

"It's Sunday."

"What? Oh, he might go to church, but which one?"

"Can't help you there. Keep in touch. Say hello to Arthur and the kids." Keely hung up.

Lane watched the timer, then turned to pour milk into his coffee cup. *I wonder what it will take to get Arthur and Matt back to some kind of normal.*

×

Chris's character fired from the hip. There was a satisfying spray of blood as the target screamed and fell behind a hump of rubble.

There was fire from his right. His character grunted when he took a hit in his Kevlar vest.

The pounding on the back door sounded familiar.

Chris's character was hit again. A veil of blood covered the soldier's goggles. "Shit!" Chris blinked, pressed the pause button on the remote, and left his perch on the footstool.

As he walked into the kitchen, his feet skidded on the lime-green linoleum. He stepped down onto the landing and opened the door. A man stood on the other side of the screen door. He was at least six foot four, weighed more than two hundred pounds, and gave the impression of someone who worked outside with his hands. Chris studied the tanned face and the white scalp of a recently shaved head. "Yes?"

"Good to see you, son. Open the door."

Chris recognized the voice, locked onto the blue eyes, and reached for the catch on the screen door. "Dad?"

John A. Jones opened the screen door and pointed at Chris's ear. "What's that?"

Chris reached for his right ear and felt the stud on his right earlobe. "I . . ."

"Take it out and grab a tea towel!" John A. pushed his way inside, forced Chris to back up the stairs, and clomped into the kitchen without removing his cowboy boots.

Chris pulled out a kitchen chair and sat.

John A. asked, "Where do you keep the clippers?"

Chris kept his voice intentionally toneless. "Under the sink."

John A. moved to the sink, opened the door, and pulled out the black plastic case holding the hair clippers. He opened the box on the solid pine kitchen table Chris had bought at a garage sale.

"There are one hundred and fifty litres of nitro," Chris said.

"Where is it?" John A. plugged the clippers in.

"In fridges in the garage." Chris had a flashback. He was four years old with a red-and-white–checked tea towel around his neck. He sat in a kitchen chair as his father put one hand on the top of Chris's head and flicked on the hair clippers.

"Why fridges?" John A. flicked a switch and the clippers hummed.

"Nitro is more stable at eight degrees Celsius." Chris blinked back tears.

"Take the earring out."

Chris thought, *You take it out*. Then he reached up and pulled the earring out. He set it on the table.

"I cut my hair off as an act of humility. Losing my hair liberated me from my old life. Now I can be closer to God and further from the vanity of men. You need to lose your hair too. Then you will understand what I'm saying to you." John A. began at the top of his son's head.

Chris saw a clump of hair fall to the floor and felt the tears running down his cheeks.

"I listened to talk radio on the drive down to Calgary. Apparently a Muslim father killed his sixteen-year-old daughter not very far from here. It was a so-called honour killing," John A. said.

"Yes." *She was almost the same age as the girl you killed in our yard.*

"Then after the haircut you must take me to a paint store. A message will have to be sent that honour killings will not be tolerated by good Christians." John A. put the palm of his left hand on a patch of scalp he'd just trimmed.

Chris knew better than to ask why. "What colour?"

"Red. The colour of blood. Where do they pray? We will pay them a nocturnal visit." John A. sniffed. "After this you will take a bath. You need to get back to having a bath every day."

×

Donna rolled out from under the van, sat up, and looked at the cases of glycerine stacked against the wall. She reached for a roll of paper towels and wiped the oil from her hands. As she stood up, she heard the sound of a car door slamming. *Shit*, Donna thought.

"Donna? Where are you?"

"In here, Mom," Donna said.

A pair of purple shoes appeared at the open door of the garage. The shoes were set off by a pair of red gaucho pants and a green-and-white horizontally striped top to accessorize Stacie's five-foot-four-inch, two-hundred-pound frame. "Why are you working on that van? I thought you were a carpenter?" Stacie pushed back a wayward strand of platinum blonde hair.

Donna took a deep breath.

"How do you like my new shoes?" Stacie turned around and kicked up her right heel to reveal a white musical note inlaid in the black sole of her shoe.

Donna leaned back and put her fists against the small of her spine. "Nice, Mom, real nice."

Stacie stomped her foot on the concrete. "You could use a new pair of shoes."

"I hate shopping. You know that." Then Donna thought, *Mom, you must be the most fucking annoying person on the planet.*

Stacie sniffed. "I've called you every day this week, and you never returned my calls."

Donna felt the required guilt and realized what her mother was doing. "Stop with the guilt trip, Mom."

"What do you mean?" Stacie reached for a tissue tucked in the pocket of her gauchos.

"You know exactly what I mean." Donna leaned against the van.

"Why did you paint that?" Stacie pointed at the slogan written in reds, blues, and oranges on the side of the van.

"It's a quote." Donna walked along the side of the van and stood next to her mother on the driveway. The shade drew a sharp line across the concrete.

"Beauty could use a little help to save the world?" Stacie asked.

"It's originally from Dostoyevsky, then Solzhenitsyn wrote about it. I added my own touch."

"Who?" Stacie asked in her little-girl voice.

"A couple of Russians."

"What's it mean?" Stacie asked.

Donna shook her head. "It's about the way you feel when you buy new shoes."

"You want to go shopping, then?" Stacie asked.

"No, Mom."

"Can I take you for lunch?" Stacie asked.

Donna looked at the van. *I've got a shitload of work to do before this is ready, and Friday is almost here. Just don't let her inside. If she sees those pamphlets on the kitchen table, I'll never hear the end of it.* Donna reached for the zipper on her coveralls. "Actually, I could use a cup of coffee and one of those sandwiches from this new place in Cochrane."

"I'll drive," Stacie said.

This was a big mistake, Donna thought fifteen minutes later as they approached Cochrane from the east along the four-lane section of the highway. She looked over her shoulder at the front bumper of the red pickup trailing them. Donna could see the truck's chrome grille, its bush guard, the winch, and the front plate that said MOVE OVER. Stacie was driving in the left lane alongside a minivan doing the speed limit.

"I don't know why he's following so close." Stacie looked at her speedometer. "I'm doing the speed limit."

Donna leaned forward to look in the side mirror. The truck was so close that she couldn't see the line of Sunday drivers following her mother's car, but Donna knew they were there.

"Motherfucker!" Stacie lifted her left hand out the window and gave the trucker a one-finger salute as he passed on the left-hand shoulder. His far wheels kicked up a cloud of pea-sized gravel and dirt that spattered Stacie's vehicle.

"No one would believe you teach kindergarten. Besides, the driver can't see you. His truck is too tall."

The truck cut in front of them and farted a black cloud of diesel smoke.

"I don't like that over there." Stacie pointed at the extraction plant with its smoke stacks and flashing lights. "It's too close to the city."

Twenty minutes later they sat at a table near the window at Guy's in Cochrane. The inside was a colour somewhere between yellow and orange — fall's deepest shade. The ceiling was curved around the counter and over the glass display where desserts and bread were lit up like precious metals in a jewellery store.

A waitress brought their Sasquatch bread sandwiches and vanilla lattes. "Enjoy," she said as she left.

Stacie lifted one half of her turkey sandwich and took a bite. "How come this is such a honky town?"

Donna choked on her coffee, reached for a napkin, and wiped her chin. "Mom, keep your voice down."

Stacie looked around. "Am I wrong?"

Donna looked around at the white faces in the crowd and shook her head. "No."

"I like Calgary. Remember my friend Harvinder? I miss her. I don't understand why she died of cancer and I survived. She had the prettiest skin. There was gold in it. I like that, you know. I like colours." Stacie swallowed and took another bite of Sasquatch.

Too bad you have no idea which ones work with the others when you mix and match clothes and shoes.

"It bothers me here." Stacie dropped her voice to a whisper. "It bothers me that there are so many crackers in this town. So many rednecks with their big pickup trucks."

Donna looked around and saw that no one was paying them any attention. "Mom, you just can't say that kind of stuff. Besides, you're as white as anyone else in here. Next time I'll take you out for a falafel on Main Street."

"What's a falafel?"

"Mediterranean food. Fresh vegetables. Great bread." Donna took a bite of sandwich.

"You mean lesbian food?"

I can't believe I came from your vagina, Donna thought. "No. Lebanese. It's run by a Lebanese guy."

"I hate it when you roll your eyes like that. I've never

had Lebanese food before." Stacie wiped her lips with a napkin.

"Beats the hell out of haggis, Mom."

"That's not saying much. Everything tastes better than haggis."

"Can we talk about something else?"

"Okay, then." Stacie leaned forward. "What are those vans for? You think I'm blind? You think just because I say stupid stuff, I can't see that you're up to something? Lisa's anniversary is coming up. You're going to make some kind of statement. What is it?"

Donna looked past her mother, realized she'd been set up, and peered through the window. "Nothing."

"You think I'm going to sit around, act like nothing is going on, pretend I don't see that you're planning something big for the anniversary of her death, pretend just so that we can be polite?" Stacie put her sandwich down, picked up her coffee, and blew steam across the top. "I'm not pretending anymore. I know we're not very close, but you're still my daughter. I know you laugh at the way I dress, and the way I buy more shoes and purses than I need, and all the stupid shit I say. I also know you better than anyone alive. I used to rely on Lisa to let me know what was going on with you. Now Lisa is gone. You think I'm gonna give up on you?"

"No, Mom, I don't think you're ever gonna give up on me. And nothing is going on." Donna set her sandwich down.

"I can always tell when you're lying. Are you building a bomb?"

Donna rolled her eyes and felt sweat gathering under her breasts. "Christ, you are a huge pain in the ass!"

"Well, at least we're being honest with each other now!" Stacie stood up and left the restaurant.

✕

Lane sat in front of his computer in the office he now shared with Nigel. Through the glass he saw he had the entire place to himself. He looked at his computer screen and a recent photo of John A. Jones. Then he looked at the photo with Chris Jones. Lane's phone rang. He checked the number. "What's up, Keely?"

"Another piece of the Jones puzzle, and a break for us, I think. An Edmonton driver was pulled over for speeding. His licence plate is registered to John A. Jones. The driver claimed to know nothing about it. My guess is that Jones switched plates to make it harder for us to identify his vehicle. I'll send you the stolen plate number and get the word out."

"Jones is here," Lane said.

"Is that your intuition speaking?" Keely asked.

"Partly." Lane studied the face of John A. Jones on his computer screen.

"And?" Keely asked.

"His son Chris is here. His wife is dead. His community fell apart. Jones has a history of moving on when things don't work out for him. And he thinks the oil industry is responsible for his wife's cancer. He's a suspect in a series of bombings. The ingredients for a bomb are most probably in Chris's hands. I get the feeling that John A. has little to lose and wants to make a big splash. The big oil companies have their offices here. It's Stampede week — you know, the greatest outdoor show on earth. Jones knows how to make headlines, and he's the kind of guy who likes to see his face on TV or the front page."

"The big question is what is his target. If we know that, we can get ahead of him," Keely said.

"It will definitely be an attack on oil and gas holdings. Oscar Mendes was a welder, so he may have been building some kind of container for a bomb. I've been doing some research on the missing chemicals and the process used to make nitroglycerine. It's more stable when it's kept cool. That means it would need a very specific kind of container made of stainless steel. Mendes was probably killed because he figured out that Jones was making a bomb and he wanted nothing to do with it." Lane looked at a map with the locations of the bombings around Lac La Biche.

"You want to meet for a bite? You're already helping to fill in some of the gaps for me. Maybe we can help each other out some more," Keely said.

"Sure. I'll call Nigel, and we can talk with someone else I've been meaning to see. By the way, do you have a description of Jones's truck?"

"Let's see. Here we go. Red Chrysler four-door pickup with a diesel engine," Keely said.

They met an hour later at the Lucky Elephant restaurant. The windows were painted with cowboys roping calves, cowboys riding broncs, and cowboys in chuckwagons.

Inside, the restaurant doors and windows were framed with rough-cut planks.

Lane saw Nigel and Keely were already sitting across from one another. He sat down between them. "Where's Uncle Tran?"

Nigel smiled. "He's at the Stampede."

"You're kidding." Lane nodded a thank-you as the waiter put a glass of water and menu in front of each of them.

Nigel said, "No, not a bit. He's a huge Stampede fan. Has the boots and hat to prove it. Even drives a pickup. Pearl — she's a seamstress — makes his tailored western shirts. Stampede is Uncle Tran's Christmas. This year the family bought him a pass so he could see all of the grandstand shows and rodeo events. He even got to ride on a float in the parade. Most of the people he helped to start over in Canada are doing well now, so they got together and bought him the gift."

The waiter took their orders and left.

Lane smiled as he imagined Uncle Tran the cowboy at the Stampede.

"He talks about the rodeo horses all the time. It's like they're his kids," Nigel said.

Lane turned to Keely. "How's your brother?"

"He sold the restaurant and went into business with a couple of his friends. And he has a new girlfriend. How's your clan?"

"Christine and Dan are hardly there, Matt is depressed— I think it's a kind of post-traumatic stress thing after being kidnapped—and Arthur has become a cancer victim instead of a survivor."

Nigel stared open mouthed at Lane.

Keely smiled.

"What's funny about that?" Lane asked.

"You'll find a way to fix it," Keely said.

"I had no idea things were so rough for you right now. How do you keep your personal life and work separate?" Nigel asked.

"I don't." Lane laughed.

"Satay beef noodle soup?" the waiter asked.

Nigel pointed at Lane.

Keely breathed in the plate of satay chicken and salad rolls that was put in front of her. "I've really missed this place."

Nigel inhaled the air above his barbecued chicken over noodles. "Comfort food."

"What's our next move?" Lane spooned a mouthful of broth and waited for the spicy heat to reach his toes.

"Find the Jones boys," Nigel said.

"Track the glycerine," Keely said.

"What about finding their target? I'd like to get ahead of the Joneses." Lane's phone rang. He checked the call display before answering. "Colin?"

"It appears the manager at Foothills Fertilizers was right about the amount of missing nitric acid," Fibre said.

"And?" Lane asked.

"We moved very quickly on this one. You should assume that you are looking for as much as one hundred and fifty litres of nitroglycerine. We confirmed that fifty litres of nitric acid are missing from Foothills Fertilizers," Fibre said.

"How did you know this case was high priority?" Lane asked.

"The amount of man power applied to this case is out of proportion with an ordinary case."

"How are the triplets?" Lane asked.

"Very fine." Fibre hung up.

"What's up?" Nigel asked.

Lane picked up his chopsticks. "We are looking for a very big bomb."

As they worked out the details of dividing up various tasks related to the investigation, Lane's phone rang again. He pulled it out of his pocket and looked at the number. "Lane."

"Miguel Sanchez called for you and asked that you meet with him," the dispatcher said.

Lane listened to the message, pressed end, and looked at Nigel. "We have to go. You coming, Keely?"

She shook her head as she finished chewing. "I've got to get back. Let me know what you find out."

Nigel drove them out of the city centre, west along the river, then north and west along Crowchild Trail. Lane sat back and enjoyed the quiet as he wondered what Miguel wanted to talk with them about.

As they approached Nose Hill Drive, Lane turned to Nigel. "How come so quiet?"

"Keely said I should listen more and talk less," Nigel said.

"You're kidding." *She never was the kind to hold back when she had something on her mind.*

Nigel shook his head. "Nope." He turned left. "Where is the Tim Hortons?"

"Just look for the traffic jam."

They parked across the street from the Tim Hortons. At least twenty-five vehicles were lined up for the drive-thru.

They found Miguel inside. He sat next to another man who wore a T-shirt and jeans. Miguel recognized the detectives and gave them a nervous smile. The other man looked around and checked for the exits.

"*Hola*," Nigel said.

"*Esto es Enrique*," Miguel said.

Nigel shook hands with Enrique. "*Mucho gusto.*"

The rest of the conversation took place in rapid-fire Spanish. Lane studied Miguel and Enrique, who was reluctant to make eye contact with the older detective.

Lane estimated that Enrique was at least a foot taller than Miguel and had longer, finer facial features than his round-faced friend. Enrique looked directly at Nigel as he spoke and would tap his index finger on the table whenever he had a point to make.

Nigel held up his hand and looked at Lane. "These guys need a couple of double-doubles and BLT sandwiches."

Lane felt his eyebrows rising.

Nigel blushed. "It's kind of good manners. They're doing us a big favour. We need to show some appreciation. It'll be an icebreaker."

Lane went up to the counter and returned with the sandwiches and four cups of coffee.

Miguel and Enrique smiled, pried open their coffee lids, and dug into the sandwiches.

While they ate, Nigel said, "Enrique was Oscar's cousin. He says he saw Chris Jones going into a paint store just up the street about an hour ago."

Lane stood up. Enrique and Miguel looked up in alarm.

Nigel said, "Enrique watched him leave in a red pickup truck. He even gave me the licence number."

Lane sat down and smiled at Miguel and Enrique.

"Enrique said that Chris Jones found out Oscar was a welder. Chris would drive him up north to do jobs at his father's place. Oscar was doing one last job for them before he went back home. Oscar told Enrique that the Joneses figured Oscar couldn't understand English and wouldn't figure out what they were doing. Enrique says that Chris worked somewhere in Calgary and would take Oscar up north for a week at a time. Oscar didn't like working for the father, but the money was good." Nigel tapped numbers and letters into his phone and waited a moment. "The plate Enrique gave us is a match to the stolen plate from Edmonton."

"Ask Enrique what Oscar thought about John A. Jones. His impressions," Lane said.

Nigel asked the question.

Enrique shook his head. "*Loco*."

Nigel said, "Crazy."

Lane thought, *I know* some *Spanish! Give me a little credit.*

Then Enrique began to talk again, too fast for Lane to follow.

When the Latino finished, Nigel said, "Oscar told Enrique that the older man with the white hair was very friendly at first. He became suspicious when Oscar made a mistake and answered a question in English. That happened about a month ago. Oscar said that more and more the old man became like a *jefe*. He ordered Oscar around and was always trying to trick him into answering questions in English. And Oscar was really upset when the *jefe*—apparently that's what Oscar always called John A. Jones—made threats to two of the women. Oscar thought Jones was especially cruel and demeaning to the women."

Lane said, "We need to get to the paint store."

Nigel thanked the men and got their phone numbers. They shook hands, and the detectives left.

The paint store was on one corner of an intersection and across the street from a car dealership. Nigel eased the Chev into a narrow space in front of the store, and they went inside. The store was brightly decorated with tasteful hues. There was a wall of colour samples on the left. In front of the samples was a table where a couple sat pointing at various shades.

A black-haired woman of about twenty-five looked over her shoulder at the detectives as they entered. She wore a blue apron that was spattered stylishly with reds and yellows. "Can I help you?"

Lane said, "Two men came in earlier. They were driving a red pickup. We have a photograph." He reached into his pocket and pulled out his ID.

The young woman asked, "Were they bald?"

Nigel said, "Yes."

Lane frowned.

"I forgot to tell you," Nigel said.

"Just a moment. Ramona!" The black-haired woman ducked out of sight into the back of the store.

Lane followed her around the counter and into the back where he came upon a woman who was somewhere between forty and fifty with her red hair tied into a ponytail. She was using a rubber mallet to seal a four-litre can of paint.

"Watch yourself. You wouldn't want to get paint on those nice clothes. Besides, customers aren't allowed back here," the redhead said. The younger woman stood behind her.

"Ramona?" Lane asked.

"That's right." Ramona pushed a wayward strand from her eyes. She wore a blue apron and shirt like the other woman. Her blue eyes studied the two men. "You're here to ask me about the father and son with the shaved heads?"

"That's right," Lane said.

"Can I see some ID?" Ramona asked. While Nigel reached for his identification, she looked at the other woman. "Go ahead, Sarah. We'll be fine here."

Sarah nodded, turned, and walked back to the front of the store.

Ramona sat on a stool next to a wooden bench, which was spattered with more colours of paint than were on display in the front of the store. "You don't mind if I sit."

Lane recognized that she hadn't asked a question. *Just get to the point with her.* He pulled out the photo of the Jones clan in front of the log house. "Were any of these people in your store today?"

"I thought I recognized him." She pointed at John A. Jones with long hair. "He's the guy from up north who's fighting with the oil and gas companies. That one could have been the kid who was with him." She pointed at Chris's image.

"What did they want?" Nigel asked.

Ramona looked directly at Nigel and smiled. "Paint." She waited a moment, then added, "And a brush."

Nigel began to speak. Lane stopped him with a let-me-handle-this-one glance. "Would you be able to share your impressions of these two?"

Ramona looked at Lane as she played with the gold cross she wore on a chain at her jugular notch. He felt an inexplicable urge to cup his hands over his balls.

"Both were bald. The older one had a tanned face, but his scalp was white. He did all of the talking. He noticed my cross and said, 'I noticed the awards on your wall. Are the awards a show of pride or were they earned in the name of the Lord?'"

Lane waited. Nigel frowned.

"How did you respond to that?" Lane asked.

"I asked him what kind of paint he wanted." She smiled at Lane.

Lane thought, *Enough of this.* "How hard do I have to work for this? We're here because it's important. It's pretty obvious that you want to put us in our place because we had the balls to come back here. The fact is we're short on time, this is important, and we could sure use some answers."

Ramona straightened her back and stared at Lane before she asked, "What is the older one's name?"

"John A. Jones," Lane said.

She nodded. "He's the kind of man who likes to put women in their place. He got my back up. So much so that I had to come back here to cool off. He's not like those missionary guys who come in here in their black suits and white shirts. There's no hint of civility with Jones. I am a woman; therefore, I need to understand I'm in the company of my superior. I've met more than a few like him in my time." She made eye contact with Lane. "He really pissed me off."

"What else is pissing you off?" Lane asked.

"Shafina was a friend of my daughter," Ramona said.

"Shafina Abdula?" Nigel asked.

Ramona nodded. "She was three months pregnant. Her father killed her because of it."

"Honour killing," Nigel said.

"What's honourable about killing your child and grandchild?" Ramona asked.

"Not much. Can you tell us anything else about Jones and his son? How did they pay for the paint? What colour did they buy?" Lane asked.

"The son is afraid of the father. They paid cash for two litres of red paint and a brush."

"Anything else?" Lane asked.

"He came in here, you know," Ramona said.

"Who do you mean?" Lane asked.

"Shafina's father came to this store two months ago. He said that my daughter and I had no morals, that we were a bad influence on his daughter. That we were to stay away from her. Dealing with Jones today was much the same as dealing with Shefic Abdula. Same misogyny. Same arrogance. John A. Jones and Shefic Abdula have the same personalities." Ramona stood up and shook her head. "It infuriates me that so many people suffer because of zealots like those two."

When they got inside the Chev, Nigel put his hands on the wheel and turned to Lane. "How come I shut her down but you were able to get her to talk?"

Lane thought for a minute. "You come on like an alpha male. Ramona is the type of person who automatically gets her back up with that kind of approach. Me, well, women usually sense that I'm less of a threat. I showed her we had a reason for being there that had very little to do with her and made her understand we needed her help."

"Oh." Nigel started the engine.

×

Donna was on her knees fitting a twenty-seven-millimetre piece of oak trim into place on the floor next to the pantry door of the kitchen. She eased her air nailer into position and pressed the trigger. A single nail sucked the oak into position. The dab of silicon on the back of the oak held it snug to the wall.

"We were just in the neighbourhood," Del said.

Without turning around Donna replied, "I hope you brought a coffee with you."

"Actually we brought something better than coffee," a woman's voice said.

Donna leaned back, felt her butt touch her heels, and stood up. "Hello, Sue."

Susan stood next to Del. She was as tall as he was but with a dancer's physique, black hair, and a baby on her hip. Fran was round faced and mostly bald, with the first hint of black hair at the sides of her head. She held a bottle in her hands and studied Donna with her large brown eyes.

Del handed Donna a blended yogurt and strawberry drink. "Thanks."

"Looks perfect as always." Del surveyed the custom kitchen.

"It's seven on a Sunday. Do you ever take a day off?" Sue asked.

Fran took the bottle from her mouth, pointed, and said something unintelligibly intelligent.

Donna looked at Sue and then at Del. *Ask them,* she thought. She felt like a pair of hummingbirds was fighting in her belly. *Ask them now or you never will.*

"What is it?" Sue asked.

So Donna asked them.

chapter 6

Vigil Marks Anniversary of Sanjiv Mohammed's Death

Demonstrators carried placards in front of the houses of parliament in Ottawa on Saturday to mark the death of the woman called Sanjiv with two minutes of silence.

Ten years ago today, Sanjiv Mohammed was stoned to death in Qatar after being convicted of adultery. Sanjiv was forty at the time of her death.

Numerous appeals from the Canadian federal government and Amnesty International failed to save Sanjiv from the executioners, who insisted it was their right under Sharia law to stone the woman.

A non-denominational gathering of human rights groups came together to raise awareness of the plight of women in developing countries. Fatima Shakir, spokesperson for Amnesty International, opened the ceremony, saying, "We remember Sanjiv in the hope that girls and women will have a future free of ignorance and oppression."

To this day, Sanjiv's son, Abraham Mohammed of Ottawa, insists that his mother was murdered because she wanted to divorce her husband. He says, "My mother's confession was the result of a week of torture and threats to her children." Abraham has no contact with his father.

Lori stood in the middle of Lane and Nigel's open door. "Mornin', boys."

They looked up in time to see a metre-long sausage-shaped bubble floating over their heads.

Lori's face was distorted behind a second soap bubble. She blew gently until the second bubble grew to the size of a basketball. It hung in the air between her and the detectives.

The sausage bubble burst. Lane flinched at the soap and water splattered across his desk.

Lori reached a long yellow wand into a crystal vase and pulled out another film-coated window that she swept into a perfect ball. "Happy birthday to you!"

"Who?' Lane asked.

Nigel blushed. "How did you know?"

The basketball bubble floated up against their window.

"I have my sources." Lori dipped her wand into the vase. "I think I'm getting the hang of this."

"How do you make that stuff?" Nigel asked.

Lori made a sweeping motion and five bubbles of diminishing size glistened about two metres above the floor. "Secret recipe."

Lane looked at Lori as a memory knocked at a closed door. *There's that huge gas plant on the west side of town.*

"Come on, tell me. It's my birthday," Nigel said.

Lori's phone rang. She set the vase and wand on Nigel's desk. "Here, play with this, birthday boy. The secret ingredient is glycerine."

Nigel looked at Lane. "No one's remembered my birthday like that since my mom died."

Six hours later, Lane looked up from his computer screen and had nine probable targets for the Joneses' bomb.

Nigel stood up. "I'm going for a run. My brain is turning into froth."

Lane looked at the picture of an extraction plant outside

the western border of the city. *It fits the geography of where Jones appears to be located. An explosion could create a toxic cloud, but the winds would have to be from the west.*

An e-mail message from Keely popped onto his screen. "Thought you might want to see this video." Lane opened the attachment, waited for it to load, then adjusted the volume.

John A. Jones crouched, resting on his heels, and held a garden hose in his right hand. Behind him were several rows of knee-high potato plants. Jones lifted the hose and looked into the camera. Water appeared to be running from the end of the hose.

Jones said, "An oil and gas exploration company has been fracking near my land. The fracking process has created cracks in the rock under my property." He took a lighter in his right hand, flicked the wheel with his thumb, and touched the flame near the end of the hose. The lighter ignited a metre-long tongue of flame.

The camera zoomed in to a close-up on Jones's face. "Would you drink this?" The camera closed in on Jones's eyes. "The oil companies poisoned my land and gave my wife cancer. When will they be brought to justice?"

The video ended.

Lane typed in the address for the Environment Canada weather forecast.

Forty minutes later he opened the front door of his house. Roz did not scamper up to greet him. Instead, there was quiet. There were no shoes on the throw rug. He slipped off his shoes and went upstairs. The door to his bedroom was open and the bed was made.

He went downstairs. Matt's door was open. His bed was unmade and empty.

The phone rang. Lane walked into the family room and picked it up.

Arthur asked, "Can you come to the vet's?"

"Why?" Lane asked.

"Just come." Arthur hung up.

There's hope in his voice, Lane thought and felt unusually optimistic as he put on his shoes, opened the front door, and locked it behind him.

The vet's clinic was next to a walk-in medical clinic and along the north side of a strip mall. Lane opened the door and was greeted by an antiseptic smell and the smile of Jessica, the receptionist. She pointed to her left.

Lane saw Arthur and Matt holding a black, gold, and white puppy. Dan and Christine were on their knees with Roz sitting between them.

An exceptionally fit and trim woman said, "This must be him."

Matt looked in Lane's direction. "This lady is giving away puppies. This one is named Scout."

Scout! The name froze Lane in a no-man's land at the centre of the waiting area.

"Cool coincidence, don't you think?" Matt asked.

Lane had a flashback of their golden retriever with its coat burned off, its skin black against the snow. His nose filled with the stink of burnt hair and flesh.

The lady said, "I wanted to meet the whole family before I give him away. I promised my daughter I'd find a good home for this one. The father was a border collie and the mother was a German shepherd. She ended up having the pups in our Quonset. The kids wanted to keep them, but we already have three dogs."

"Well?" Christine asked.

Lane thought about double the dog shit in the backyard, walking two dogs, and training this puppy. Then he looked at the faces watching him. He saw the hopeful smile on Arthur's face. "Can I see him?"

Matt stood up and set Scout on the chair. The pup had

one ear up and the other down. His chest was white and his back was black. Lane picked up one of the pup's paws. He pressed in between Scout's toes — a trick he remembered from his grandfather, who showed him that he could test a dog's temperament by the way it reacted to having its feet handled. Scout licked Lane's hand. *Maybe a puppy will cheer things up around the house*. Lane looked at the woman and asked, "Can we have a minute, please?"

Lane looked at Matt and Arthur. "I'm saying yes. Will you do something for me?"

"What?" Matt asked and crossed his arms as his defences went up.

He knows what I'm going to ask. Don't mess this up, Lane looked at Matt, then at Arthur. "I want the two of you to see Dr. Alexandre."

Matt frowned.

Arthur rubbed the puppy behind the ears.

"Which two do you mean?" Christine asked.

"Matt and Arthur," Lane said.

"Okay," Arthur said.

"And I want all of you to walk Scout at least once a day," Lane said.

"Is this blackmail?" Matt asked.

"I've already said yes," Lane said.

"Will you clean up the shit?" Matt asked.

"If Dan and Christine help," Lane said.

"He's already house trained," Arthur said.

"Matt?" Lane asked.

"Okay," Matt said.

"Christine? Dan?" Lane asked.

"As long as we get to walk Roz too," Dan said.

"It's a deal, then?" Lane asked.

chapter 7

Record Day for Stampede Attendance

Clear skies and 30-degree temperatures have resulted in a record day for Stampede attendance.

The Stampede grounds are overflowing with visitors. Vendors are smiling, and suppliers are scrambling to keep up with demands for all manner of food and refreshments.

Local restaurant managers have never seen anything like it. Maddy Preston of the Avenue Diner says, "We usually slow down between ten in the morning and noon and for an hour or two after the lunch crowd leaves. It's not happening this week. We go steady until closing time."

Hotels are filled to capacity. Bars are the same. "We're having a tough time keeping up with the demand for beer and spirits," says Raoul Mendez, manager of Cowboys, one of Calgary's most popular bars.

The forecast calls for blue skies and warm temperatures until at least Friday.

"Is it straight?" John A. Jones finished the last letter of the first word on the cedar siding above the windows at the Ranchlands Islamic Centre.

Chris stepped back from holding the bottom of the ladder. He looked up at the first word. It was difficult to read because the single lamp illuminating the strip mall's parking lot was about forty metres away. The streetlamp was a little closer, but its light was aimed away from the Centre. "It looks good."

John A. leaned right and began to paint the letter B.

Chris looked over his shoulder as a car drove past. The street was a good three metres lower than the parking lot, so there was little chance of them being spotted at three thirty in the morning. He went back to steadying the ladder.

"It finally cooled off a bit. God is making it easier for us to do His work." John A. looked down at his son. "My namesake believed in the supremacy of the white race. Sir John A. was a wise man."

Chris looked at the vehicles left overnight by people who'd decided not to drive after drinking.

Paint splattered on the sidewalk. "Take the screwdriver and get a new licence plate for my truck," John A. said.

Chris reached into the side pocket of his jeans and walked toward a white Escalade.

✕

There was dew on the windshield when Lane climbed into the passenger seat of the Jeep. It was five o'clock, the sun was beginning to rise in a clear sky, and the air held the promise of a hot, dry day.

Matt got in behind the wheel, put the key in the ignition, and started the engine. When he reached the T intersection at the bottom of the hill, he put on his right signal, then looked right and left.

Lane put his hand on Matt's shoulder. "Turn left, please."

"I thought you wanted a ride to the LRT station. I don't want to be late for work," Matt said.

"You go ahead." Lane undid his seat belt and opened the door.

"What are you doing?" Matt looked at Lane, then looked left.

Lane pointed at the front wall of the Islamic Centre. A message was painted in red. The letters were a metre high: YOUR BLOOD: AN UNQUENCHABLE THIRST.

"Your bloob?" Matt asked.

"I think that he put a colon inside of the D," Lane said.

"He? You know who did this?" Matt asked.

Lane pulled his phone out and nodded. "I've got a pretty good idea. You go ahead. I need to call this in. I'll catch a ride downtown with a uniform." He stepped out of the Jeep, closed the door, and began to dial as Matt drove west to work.

Within thirty minutes the Forensic Crime Scene Unit had arrived. Black-and-white police cars blocked both ends of the lot.

Colin Weaver climbed out of the passenger seat of the unit's cab. He maneuvered himself into his white bunny suit, boots, and hood and then asked, "What am I doing here? I don't usually get called to investigate graffiti."

Lane thought, *Remember, it's Fibre who's asking.* "There is evidence to suggest that the pair with the nitroglycerine has done this. So far, we haven't been able to track them. One is a suspect in a series of oil and gas sabotages. We need anything you can find at the scene that might help us track him."

Fibre thought for a moment, then stood next to Lane and looked at the scene. He pointed at the words written above the windows of the Islamic Centre. "He used a ladder. There will be spatter. Perhaps there will be some footprints or handprints." Fibre moved to the back of the unit, opened the door, and pulled out his kit.

Lane turned around and watched the traffic rolling by. The volume was picking up as people headed to work. *Jones is the kind of man who would like to see how his work has been received*. He watched for a red pickup truck and kept his ears tuned for a diesel engine.

Fifteen minutes later, a pickup approached from the west. It slowed. Lane recognized Donna at the wheel. He waved. She waved back and continued toward the traffic lights.

Lane looked at the open-air rink across the street and then at the tree-covered hill behind it. *A good place to watch what's going on.*

He stepped carefully down a sloped retaining wall of river rock and crossed the street.

A grey Chev pulled up and parked on the wrong side of the street. Nigel opened his window. "What's up?"

Lane turned, crouched on the grass, and put his hands on the sill of the open car window. "I want you to look directly at me."

Nigel blinked and kept his eyes focused on Lane.

"I'd like you to drive up into the lot on your right. Park near the pub. Then I want you to walk through that narrow passageway next to the pub like you're going to the convenience store for a couple of coffees. Instead walk south, cross the street, and come around the school to the field at its south end. I'm going up the hill to the south to see whether anyone is in the trees watching what's going on at the Islamic Centre."

"Want me to alert the uniforms?" Nigel asked.

"No. That would be too obvious, and it could scare these guys off. I want to keep them in place for as long as possible." Lane stood up, turned, and walked through an opening in the fence. He walked along the west end of the paved outdoor rink. Then he turned right along the edge of the trees until he reached a pathway that went straight up the north face of the hill.

He kept his eyes on the trail and forced himself to look neither right nor left. He reached the top and a plateau. He worked his way to the crest of the next hill and looked down on the school field.

Nigel waved at him from the east side of the school where he was out of sight.

Lane's phone vibrated. "Yes?"

"Three guys crossed the field and went into those condos behind the other strip mall," Nigel said.

Lane looked at the condos. A church steeple was visible behind the condos. "Call the uniforms to watch the four exits from Ranchlands. They're looking for a late-model red Chrysler pickup. It may have another plate by now." Lane hung up and scanned the neighbourhood from his vantage point. To the east and across the street from the schoolyard was another treed park left to grow wild. *If he's watching me, he's watching from there.* He stepped back from the crest of the hill and moved behind the trees. He walked down a slope that was used for tobogganing in the winter. Trees lined either side and would provide cover until he reached the school.

✕

"I should have brought the .30-30," John A. Jones said. He stood next to Chris atop the hill across the street from the schoolyard and in front of an apartment building.

Chris thought, *I thought the Bible said thou shalt not murder.* "You brought it with you?"

His father turned and looked down at his son. "Of course."

They can use it to tie you to two murders, Chris thought.

"I have the right to defend myself."

Against an unarmed girl and a man running away from you? Chris thought.

"That one who was on top of the hill. He's getting closer. I may have to put him down."

"How do you know he's getting closer?" Chris asked.

"I know. Just like I know many other things. God warns me when a threat is nearby. That one is a threat." John A. pointed at Lane, who appeared around the south corner of the school.

Mom always said, 'Just agree with him. He has trouble with contradiction.'

John A. continued. "We'd better get back to the house and put that new plate on my truck. We need to get both vehicles in the garage."

Chris reached into the pocket of his pants, pulled out the two screws he'd taken from the car, and dropped them on the ground before following his father down the hill.

✕

Three minutes later, Lane reached the spot where John A. and Chris Jones had been. He looked across at the crest of the hill he'd stood on a few minutes before. He heard footsteps and looked over his shoulder.

Nigel asked, "Find anything?"

Lane held up two screws.

"What are those?" Nigel asked.

"We need to check whether one of the cars in the parking lot is missing a licence plate."

It took them ten minutes to make it back to the Islamic Centre. A quick survey of the vehicles parked near the pub revealed the Escalade with a missing plate.

"We need that plate number because it'll probably end up on Jones's pickup truck." Lane turned to Nigel.

"I'll get right on it." Nigel fished his phone out of his pocket and walked forward to check the Escalade's VIN.

✕

John A. Jones slid out of the cab through the passenger door of his red truck. "We need to stay out of sight for the next few days." The door of his truck bumped up against the side of Chris's truck. John A. leaned the passenger seat forward and pulled out his Winchester .30-30 in its green rifle case. He closed his door. "Don't worry. A little mark won't hurt your truck. There won't be much left of it by the end of this week anyways."

"Why wait that long?" Chris stood at the door connecting the house and garage.

"I've been watching the weather forecast. Clear and calm 'til the end of the week. The winds should pick up from the west by Friday or Saturday. A good, strong, steady wind is what we're going to need." John A. closed the door, held the rifle out front, and eased between the trucks.

Chris stepped into the garage and opened the first fridge to check the temperature of the nitro.

"Is it okay?" John A. asked.

Chris nodded. "Yep. Right where it should be." *What do we need that rifle in the house for?*

"The only problem is we need to get some groceries," John A. said.

"No worries. I'll phone an order in and have it delivered." Chris took his time closing the fridge door.

chapter 8

Local MLA Speaks Out on Honour Killing Legislation

MLA Laura Poulin promises to introduce a private member's bill at the Alberta Legislature this fall.

Poulin says, "We need to protect young women from parents who adhere to rules that restrict girls' and women's right to religious and personal freedoms."

Poulin would not get into specifics about the wording of the legislation.

Poulin says, "A young woman at my son's school was murdered by her father and brother. This government has a responsibility to make it clear that so-called honour killings will not be tolerated in this province. We need to protect the rights and freedoms women have enjoyed for generations in this country."

Bryan Kowalewski, leader of the opposition, says, "Poulin's proposed bill exploits a tragedy. In fact, her bill may do nothing to help the very people it pretends to protect. My party will be proposing more effective legislation in the fall."

"What's our worst-case scenario?" Harper sat at a conference table with Lane, Keely, Nigel, and Harold Smith, the fire chief. Harold was balding, grey haired, and lantern jawed. His uniform jacket hung on the back of his chair.

"As far as an explosion goes, it depends where detonation occurs. You might be lucky and have only broken windows if there are any buildings close by. If the explosion happens near a hospital or shopping mall, the casualties could be in the hundreds. If we have a toxic cloud induced by the explosion, casualties could be even higher. We've had some experience with an explosion and fire at an oil-recycling plant in August of 1999. It was inside the city limits, there were only two fatalities, but there were evacuations." Harold looked around the table. "That was not a deliberate act. You're talking about a deliberate act. Casualties will most likely be much higher."

"That's right," Harper said.

"Any sense of the target?" Harold asked.

Nigel said, "It will most likely be a petroleum facility. The guy we're dealing with blames his wife's cancer death on oil and gas activities around their home near Lac La Biche. He is a suspect in previous bombings of pipelines and sour-gas installations. Recently he has been saying that the only way people in the cities will understand what's going on in rural areas is if they are exposed to the same poison."

Harold said, "If it is a petroleum facility like an extraction plant, then we have a real problem. Some of the gases those facilities produce are heavier than air. I wouldn't want to think about the scope of the disaster if a toxic, heavier-than-air gas is released by an explosion."

Harper looked sideways at Nigel, gave him a warning glare, and turned to Lane. "How sure are you that Jones is in town?"

"Two independent eye witnesses identified John A. Jones on Sunday," Lane said.

Harper stared out the window. "Then we have to hunt the son of a bitch down." He turned again to Lane. "What do you need?"

✕

Donna had finished one house and was on her way to her next job. Norah Jones was playing on the truck's radio when she decided she would stop at home to freshen up and have lunch.

She drove west along John Laurie Boulevard. At the first intersection into Hawkwood, she pulled up behind three media SUVs at the red light. The vehicles had call signs in metre-high letters painted along their sides. The light turned green. They proceeded west and at the first intersection beyond the Eagle's Nest turned north toward the church. She spotted a white CBC van with its purple logo approaching from the other direction.

I hope things aren't about to get worse. Donna followed the procession and parked at the back of the church lot under the buzz of the power lines that stretched east and west.

A group of three women stood under the shade of an awning outside the open front doors of the church, the Rocky Mountains in the background. The women reminded Donna of lipstick, nail files, and eyeliner pencils.

The TV crews hauled cameras from their vehicles. Two reporters—one man and one woman—primped behind hand-held mirrors.

Donna opened her door and stepped out in her black T-shirt and faded bib overalls. She felt the heat of the pavement through the soles of her boots and began to walk toward the front of the church. A growing sense of apprehension made her stomach rumble. She noticed a black town car to her left.

A back door opened on the passenger side. Laura Poulin

stepped out. The ex-Stampede Princess wore a red knee-length skirt and a red fitted jacket. She flipped her blonde shoulder-length hair over her collar. Poulin nodded in the direction of the trio of women at the front of the church.

Donna caught the scent of Chanel No. 5.

The voice of the woman in the middle carried across the lot. "We've invited you here to witness a protest. We are here to say that what happened to Shafina Abdula must not happen again. What some call an honour killing dishonours women in this country and, in particular, women in this community." She held up a book with both of her hands.

Donna had a better view of the speaker now. She was taller than Poulin, wore a similar red outfit, and had styled and bleached her hair the same shade of blonde. In fact, all three of the women had similar hair and clothing styles.

"The Quran dishonours women. We are here to support the rights of all women in this country." The woman bent at the knees and moved to set the Quran on the ground. On either side, the women put their hands on the Quran and knelt.

The must have spent a lot of time rehearsing this. Donna began to move forward. "Hey!"

The women stopped before the Quran touched the ground. They looked in Donna's direction. The one in the middle continued to talk. "In this country we have the right to speak up for women who've lost their voices."

Donna was ten metres away and closing. She focused on the Quran and the women who held it about fifty centimetres from the pavement. "Do you understand that people will die if you do this?" Donna pointed to the cameras aimed at the scene. "This story will make its way around the world. If you do this, there will be blood on your hands."

"The Quran walks all over women's rights. A young girl was killed in this neighbourhood. We have every right to walk all over the Quran."

Donna stopped within a metre of the women and looked down. The cloud of Chanel No. 5 was overwhelming and made her eyes tear. She could see the layers of makeup on the women's faces, the way their eyebrows were bleached blonde like their hair. The women's eyes looked around and past Donna. *They're looking for direction from Poulin,* Donna thought.

"Women have rights in this country." The woman in the centre used both hands to bring the Quran in front of her face.

Donna grabbed the Quran with her right hand and tucked it in against her elbow.

"Give that back!" The woman's eyes were almost as wide as her mouth.

Donna sensed the cameras coming closer as she backed away. She heard the door of the town car shut. *Think fast!*

The CBC reporter, followed by the woman with the camera, approached as Donna walked toward the town car.

The reporter asked, "Donna Laughton? I've interviewed you before about your sister. She was a medic killed in Afghanistan. Are you here to support these women in their protest?"

"No. These people do not honour the memory of my sister. And they do not honour the memory of Shafina Abdula, or any other woman, for that matter. They are practising the same intolerance that killed my sister."

The reporter looked startled.

Donna heard the town car's engine roar to life.

The woman with the camera approached to get a close-up of Donna.

Donna looked over her shoulder and saw the other reporters headed her way. She stopped at the front of the town car and looked through the windshield. The driver wore a black suit jacket, white shirt, and black tie. "My sister worked to save lives. These women —" Donna pointed at the front door of the church, then at the car "— incite violence."

Another reporter asked, "Don't you think they have a right to their opinion?"

Donna smiled and looked at the black car. "Why don't you ask Laura Poulin? She's the person who orchestrated this event."

The driver of the town car inched forward. Donna stood her ground as the bumper came close to touching her knees. The driver leaned on the horn. The reporters gathered around the car with microphones and cameras.

One knocked on the town car's tinted rear window. A moment later the window hummed and opened. The reporter stuck her microphone inside the car window.

Laura Poulin spoke. "Women in this country have the right to voice an opinion even if those same rights are restricted in other parts of the world."

Donna shook her head as the cameras and reporters gathered around the open window of the town car. Poulin opened the door, stepped out, and continued. "The Charter of Rights and Freedoms guarantees our right to freedom of speech. And that book belongs to me!"

Donna turned and saw Poulin looking at her over the roof of the town car. Donna felt an old rage take hold. "What does it take for you to understand? Do you have to lose someone close first? If you disrespect this —" Donna held up the Quran "— another Shafina will die. Another Lisa will die. You will have blood on your hands no matter what you say about freedom of speech. What about another person's right to life?" She walked away from the cameras, climbed into her truck, set the Quran on the seat beside her, started the engine, and drove away.

×

John A. Jones wore sweatpants and a T-shirt. He sat in a garage-sale leather recliner and watched the weather channel.

Chris looked at the crown of his father's polished scalp.

"Is the coffee ready?" John A. asked.

"Almost," Chris replied.

"It's looking more and more like we'll leave on Friday. I don't know why the Good Lord is making us wait, but I've learned to trust in Him and do things in His time."

Chris heard the coffee machine splutter and made his way into the kitchen. As he poured his father's coffee, he thought, *Why not smash the pot over his head?*

chapter 9

Two Horses Killed in Chuckwagon Crash

Stampede officials are investigating a crash at the Stampede racetrack last night.

Two horses from the Franky Smith rig were euthanized. Veterinarians said the injuries to the horses included multiple fractures to their legs.

The collision occurred on the backstretch when the Brubecker wagon cut across to the inside of the track and forced Smith's horses into the rail.

One outrider was sent to the hospital with undisclosed injuries.

So far, there have been no other fatalities at this year's Stampede.

Heather Logan, spokesperson for PETA, says, "This happens at the Stampede every year. It's time for the chuckwagon races to stop. Haven't enough animals died in the name of entertainment?"

The howling tore Lane away from sleep. Scout, who hadn't made a sound until now, was wailing.

Lane looked toward the open bedroom window. *Did we leave the dogs outside?*

He sat up and put his feet on the hardwood floor. He pulled on a pair of sweatpants. Lane looked over at Arthur, who snored.

The dog howled.

Matt screamed. It was a savage sound, a wounded sound, a sound with a physical presence. Lane shivered, made for the door, and hit the light switch. The room filled with a blaze of white light. He opened the door and turned on the hallway light.

Matt screamed again.

Lane pounded down the stairs and into the kitchen, turning on lights as he went.

At the bottom of the next set of stairs Scout—mouth open, eyes open — howled. Roz lay with her paws over her ears. Lane's feet met the oak floor of the family room.

Matt opened his bedroom door and stood there in his black underwear. His chest heaved, his eyes wide open.

Lane saw a vein pounding at Matt's throat.

"He killed Jessica!" Matt said.

"Who?" Lane asked and, as he said it, knew the answer.

"The devil! The guy in the devil mask! He killed her!"

"What happened?" Christine wore an oversize white T-shirt and grey flannel pajama shorts. Daniel stood behind her in his blue boxers.

Thump!

They all looked at the ceiling.

"Arthur? You okay?" Lane asked.

"What's happening?" Arthur asked.

Lane turned to Matt. "Jessica is safe. You saved her yourself. It happened a year ago, remember?"

Matt dropped his chin to his chest and shook his head.

"He killed her! She was crying. He picked her up and threw her against the wall! I went to her. She wasn't breathing. Her eyes were open!"

Keep your voice low. Lane stepped closer to Matt. "It was a nightmare."

"I have to see that she's alive! I have to see that she's okay!" Matt turned his back to them and began searching the floor for his clothing.

Lane saw the sweat running down Matt's spine.

Matt went back into his room and pulled on jeans and a T-shirt. "I've gotta know."

"Matt? It's two thirty in the morning," Christine said.

Matt stood in the doorway. His face was pale against the fabric of his T-shirt. "I need to be sure!"

Give him time to wake up. To work this out on his own. Lane asked, "Can we have a cup of coffee first?"

Matt blinked. He looked at Christine and Dan. He saw Arthur at the top of the stairs. Matt leaned against the doorway. "Shit!"

Five minutes later, the warm scent of coffee filled the kitchen. Roz yawned, and her tongue curled into a C. Scout sat next to her, watched, and yawned.

Lane saw that Matt's heart rate and breathing had calmed.

After they finished their coffee, Christine and Dan went back to bed.

Arthur pointed at Matt. "Okay if you and I see Dr. Alexandre this morning?"

"I have to work." Matt got up to pour another coffee.

"You can phone in sick for one day," Lane said.

Matt turned to protest.

Lane stood up. Arthur did the same. They approached their nephew together.

Matt's chin dropped. "I can't sleep. I close my eyes and I see Jessica's body. I see the guy in the devil mask."

"Should we go for a walk?" Lane asked.

Matt nodded.

Within a few minutes, five of them stood on the sidewalk in front of the house.

"It's okay if I come, right?" Arthur asked.

Lane and Matt looked at Arthur like he'd just opened his fly to pee on the front lawn.

"Of course." Matt held out Scout's leash.

"I've been feeling left out," Arthur said.

No, you've been feeling sorry for yourself, Lane thought, then felt guilty.

"Get over it." Matt smiled.

Yes, please get over it.

Roz interrupted the conversation by pulling Lane down the sidewalk.

Scout followed, belly close to the cement, four paws clawing like he was climbing a sheer rock face.

"Wait for me," Arthur said.

They walked down the hill and past the Islamic Centre. The air was crisp and the moon full, but the roads were deserted. The lights at the intersection flashed yellow. A jackrabbit scooted across the street, and Roz hit the end of her leash. Scout sniffed the air.

"Am I going crazy?" Matt asked.

Lane answered. "No. You are, however, definitely short on sleep, and you're probably suffering from delayed stress over the kidnapping."

Roz zigged right. Scout followed.

"The nightmare was so real," Matt said.

"A better name is night terrors," Arthur said.

"What's that supposed to mean?" Matt asked.

"Just that nightmares bring your worst fears right to the very edge of reality and sometimes —" Arthur said.

"Sometimes?" Matt asked.

"— they seem to cross the line into reality."

He doesn't know about what happened to you, Arthur. Lane said, "Tell him what happened to you when you were eighteen. Just before you left home."

"When I was your age, I was hiding who I was. I was ashamed of who I was. I stuck a gun in my mouth," Arthur said.

"What happened?" Matt asked.

"Your mother talked me out of killing myself."

"She never told me that," Matt said.

"It wasn't the kind of thing we could talk about with anyone else. There would have been too many questions to answer. We got used to never saying anything about it, even to each other," Arthur said.

Roz turned right along a path that ran between fenced backyards. As they passed the various houses, no lights shone. Trees lined the other side of the pathway. They relied on the soft moonlight to illuminate the tricky humps in the pavement raised by poplar roots.

They crossed a street.

On the far side, Scout sat and refused to move. Matt tugged on the leash.

"Wait." Arthur bent to pick up the pup.

On the left side of the path was a natural area where trees and shrubs grew wild. Roz sniffed a patch of grass and squatted. They heard the gentle splatter of her urine.

×

John A. Jones sipped his coffee and stood back from the kitchen window where he could remain hidden in shadow.

He saw three silhouettes stop on the trail running along the chain-link fence that marked the eastern border of their rented backyard.

"Who goes for a walk at this hour?" He studied the silhouettes.

Lori tipped her straw hat with its rolled-up brim. "You look like shit."

Lane smiled. "You always know just what to say to cheer me up. Where did you get the hat?"

"Stole it from Leslie."

"Your daughter will miss it. It's the perfect Stampede hat." Lane drained the coffee he'd picked up on the way to work.

"Where's my coffee?" Lori asked.

Lane looked at his cup and blushed.

"Thank you."

"Are you being sarcastic?"

Lori shook her head and rolled her eyes. "For being kind to Nigel! The kid is happy now. In fact, I can't remember when he was ever this happy around here. Did you get any sleep last night?"

"Thank you for making me read the file. His behaviour makes more sense now that I know where it's coming from." Lane looked for a garbage can, tossed the cup, and missed.

"He told me he enjoys coming to work and you actually listen to what he has to say."

Unaccountably, Lane felt tears in his eyes. He bent over, picked up the cup, dropped it in the can, and wiped his eyes.

"What's going on with you?" Lori asked.

Matt has some kind of post-traumatic issue. I'm tired of Arthur playing the victim. Christine has become distant and seems to prefer Dan's family to ours. Now we have a new dog I have to take care of. To top it off, there's a guy who's probably trying to set off a bomb so he can kill thousands of people during Stampede. Lane looked her in the eye and smiled. "Nothing."

Lori barked a laugh. "Liar."

Lane smiled back and turned toward his office. "There's work to do."

Lori stood up and put her hand on Lane's shoulder. "Don't worry so much. You've been here before. Things always turn to shit before you come out smelling like —"

"A portable toilet on a hot summer afternoon?" Lane asked.

"— I was going to say like fresh coffee in the morning."

Lane laughed. His mind began to churn with new possibilities for tracking down the Joneses.

Nigel elbowed the office door open. It slapped against its stop and smacked Nigel on the left elbow.

Nigel stared the door down and rubbed his elbow with his right hand. "I think I know a way to pull this all together and track them down."

"Can you wait? We need Keely and Harper to be here."

Nigel said, "Of course. It'll give me a chance to put it all down on the computer. It came to me as I walking down the Stephen Avenue Mall this morning."

Twenty minutes later, Nigel, Lane, Keely, and Harper sat at the conference table.

Harper looked at Lane as if to say, *Face it, Nigel is a fuck-up, and it's only a matter of time before you recognize that fact.*

Keely fiddled with her phone. She kept looking at it as if willing it to ring.

Lane thought, *Nigel, if you can pull it all together, now would be a good time.*

Nigel tapped a button on his computer to project on the screen at one end of the table. An image of John A. Jones and his long white hair appeared. He held the end of a water hose and flicked a lighter. Flame shot from the end of the hose. Jones turned to the camera and said, "This is what the oil industry has done to our well water."

Nigel stopped the image and clicked on another site. This time Jones faced a camera. "Yes, a girl was shot on our land. I don't know who shot her, and I don't want to know."

Li clicked a third image. Jones wore a black suit and tie. He stared at the camera. "My wife died of cancer. As we put her body in the ground, I place the blame for her death at the feet of the oil industry. An industry based in a city filled with people who seem unaware of what oil and gas exploration does to those whose land is corrupted and whose loved ones are made sick."

Nigel let the screen go black. "Over the last ten years, there has been a series of explosions at oil and gas installations." Nigel tapped a key and a map appeared on the screen. "Each explosion occurred within a day's drive of Jones's home."

Harper took a long breath.

Nigel frowned.

Keely's eyebrows were cocked at odd angles.

Lane said, "Go on, please."

Nigel tapped another key. Another map appeared. This one was a map of Calgary's northwest quadrant. Purple dots formed a compact cluster near the intersection of Nose Hill Drive and Crowchild Trail. "These dots represent purchases of glycerine, sightings of John A. and Chris Jones, and the recent defacing of the Islamic Centre."

Another tap revealed green dots. Nigel said, "These are the locations of the receipts found on the body of Oscar Mendes." Again the dots were clustered near the same intersection.

"And these are the locations of supermarkets in the same area," Nigel said as two red dots appeared across the street from one another and next to the green and purple dots.

Harper leaned forward, studying the map intently.

"The yellow Xs represent the roadblocks set up to stop a fleeing Jones, assuming that he and his son were responsible for the words written on the Islamic Centre." Nigel tapped a final key and a yellow box appeared. Three sides of the box ran through the yellow Xs. The fourth side ran along Crow-child Trail. "It appears that we are likely to find John A. Jones within this area."

"My neighbourhood," Lane said.

"He would probably need a house with a double garage to mix the chemicals," Keely said.

"And hide his truck," Harper said.

"And they have to eat. I know that Co-Op delivers grocer-ies to your door." Lane looked at the map and checked the location of the screws he'd found on the ground in the park. Then he looked at the path he'd taken this morning walking the dogs with Matt and Arthur.

"I'm going to check with Co-Op and Safeway to see who has had food delivered to their door over the past five days," Nigel said.

"I'll work with Lori and see what we can find out about houses — at least those with garages — for rent in the neigh-bourhood," Lane said.

"I'll keep track of glycerine purchases and any of the hard-ware needed for storage and handling of the chemicals. Along with components for detonators," Keely said.

Harper said, "Lane will be the primary contact, and he'll keep me up to speed." He stood up and looked at Lane, then at Nigel.

Cam, you look puzzled, Lane thought.

"Nigel?" Harper asked.

Nigel looked up at the deputy chief.

"Good work," Harper said.

Nigel blinked and turned to Lane, who smiled back at the rookie.

Lane looked at Harper. "Nigel says thank you."

×

Matt sat next to Arthur in Dr. Alexandre's waiting room.

Arthur looked at one painting on the wall. Shades of blue behind the grey-silver of birch trees in winter.

Matt's thumbs flew over his phone as he texted then shifted back to playing a game.

"Why are you here?" Arthur asked.

Matt looked up. His eyes were red, and his hair was uncombed and unwashed. "I'm goin' crazy."

"But why?" Arthur asked.

"I can't sleep because of the nightmares. I have no appetite. It's like I'm digging a hole. It just gets deeper and darker." Matt pressed a button on his phone, then tucked it in his shirt pocket.

Arthur stared at the birch trees. "I'm tired all of the time. All I want to do is sleep. And I don't think —"

"Go on."

"— I don't think Paul loves me anymore," Arthur said.

"I've never heard you call Uncle Lane by that name."

"He doesn't like it."

"Besides that, you're being stupid," Matt said.

"How so?"

"He loves you. He's just mad at you."

"For what?"

"You really don't know?" There was a look of pure amazement on Matt's face when he turned to look at his uncle's round face.

"No, I don't know." Arthur faced his nephew. "Tell me."

"You've gone from being a cancer survivor to being a cancer victim," Matt said.

"No, I haven't!" Arthur looked away.

"Whatever."

The door to the waiting room opened. Alexandre's secretary poked his head in. "Matthew Mereli?"

Matt stood up. "I'm Matt."

"This way." The secretary smiled and held the door for him.

"No, I haven't." Arthur watched the door close.

✕

"I brought this for you." Stacie carried a case of glycerine in her hands and a new black ten-litre purse over her shoulder. "Wanna grab it?" She wore a pink top and lime-green gauchos. She crossed into the shadow inside of the garage.

Donna looked over her shoulder, spotted her mother, stepped out of the cab of the van, and hefted the case of glycerine. "Why'd you buy this?" Donna put the case atop the others against the garage wall. "Did you pay cash?"

"Why?" Stacie asked.

"Because a card can be traced."

"You never answered my question. What are you doing?" Stacie poked around the inside of her bag. She pulled out a pair of black coveralls. "Try these on. Your other ones have a hole in them. Besides, black looks better on you."

"Mom, it's only two o'clock. When did you have time to do so much shopping?" Donna reached for the black coveralls. She grabbed the shoulders, let the coveralls unfold, and was careful to hold the cuffs off the floor. "These are nice."

"Don't sound so shocked. I do know how to shop. And to answer your question, I know where to find good stuff."

Change the topic. "Can you find what's wrong under the hood of this thing? I can't get it started."

Stacie set her purse atop the cases of glycerine, followed Donna around to the front of the van, and peered at the collection of parts under the hood.

Donna went to the opposite front fender. "It should start."

Stacie grabbed a blue towel, reached over the grille, and lifted a battery cable that hung like the neck of a dead chicken. "Where does this go?"

Donna rolled her eyes, moved beside her mother, took the cable, and attached it to the battery. She eased around behind her mother, got into the cab of the van, and turned the key. The engine coughed, fired up, then purred. Donna leaned out of the cab. "Thanks, Mom!"

"Now will you tell me what you're up to?"

Donna shut off the engine. "Mom, we both know you can keep a secret for about as long as it takes to get to the nearest phone. And you spend your days with people who love to gossip."

Stacie opened her mouth to protest.

Donna held up her hand. "You're the one who told me about the way people gossip at your school, remember? Your exact words were, 'It's really quite amazing how fast a juicy bit of gossip makes it from one end of the building to the other.'"

Stacie shrugged her shoulders. "I know that what you're doing has something to do with Lisa. I want to be a part of it. I miss her too."

Donna looked at the wall and her mother's oversized purse. "To tell the truth, I could use some help. I can't drive two vans at once."

"What are you planning?"

"Will you meet me here at seven o'clock tomorrow morning?" Donna asked.

"What do I need to wear?"

"We need to go shopping for that right now." Donna unzipped the front of her coveralls.

"Shopping? Where?"

Donna smiled. "This may be the one place in this city where you've yet to shop."

"Why?"

"Do you want back in with me? Do you want us to be closer?" Donna asked.

Stacie nodded. Her eyes filled with tears.

"Then it's time to make a choice. Either you trust me or you don't." Donna shimmied her way out of the coveralls. "If you trust me, then stop asking questions and get into my truck."

✕

"Where's the milk?" There was bristle on John A. Jones's face and head. He held a cup of coffee in his right hand and held the fridge door open with his left.

"We're out," Chris said.

"What've we got?" John A. closed the fridge door.

"Not much. You told me we're leaving tomorrow and to forget about ordering more groceries."

"We need a few things now, and I'm tired of pizza."

"You want me to go to the grocery store?" Chris began to feel nervous as he recognized the signs of anxiety in his father's voice.

"No, they're watching. I can feel it. I saw one of those cops this morning." John A. opened a cupboard door and put his now empty coffee cup on the shelf.

"Where?" Chris shoved his hands into the pockets of his combat pants.

John A. cocked his head to the left. "Out there on that pathway."

"Did he see you?"

"No." John A. opened another cupboard door. He pulled out a tumbler, ran the water in the kitchen sink, and filled the glass.

"I can phone Co-Op, and they'll deliver the groceries."

"Can they trace us?" John A. asked.

"We'll pay with cash."

"But they'll know our address," John A. said.

"We've been ordering takeout pizza, and no one's come

knocking." Chris felt sweat gathering along the edge of what used to be his hairline.

"Got some paper? We need to make a list of food we can travel with so we only have to stop for gas on the way back home." John A. opened one drawer and then another.

×

Stacie looked around the showroom floor. A row of motorcycles gleamed under the spotlights. "Is this where you bought your bike?"

Donna said, "Yep."

"Hey, Donna," a woman called. She had shoulder-length black hair and wore a black T-shirt and black jeans. She walked closer.

"Carly!" Donna hugged the woman. "This is Stacie, my mom."

Carly turned to Stacie. "Good to meet you."

"My mom needs a helmet," Donna said.

"Full face?" Carly asked.

"Is there a helmet that won't mess up my hair?" Stacie asked.

"Afraid not." Carly smiled.

Stacie turned to Donna. "Why do I need a helmet?"

"It's part of the plan," Donna said.

They followed Carly toward the stairs leading to the basement. She began to hop down the stairs with one hand on the railing.

"What happened to your leg?" Stacie asked.

"Mom!" Donna said.

Carly reached the basement floor and turned to face Stacie. "I was in a motorcycle accident when I was eighteen. Lost my leg from the knee down." She lifted her right pant leg to reveal the shiny metal limb reaching out of her shoe.

"Sorry," Stacie said.

"No worries. Usually the kids ask. It's an honest question. The helmets are over here." Carly pointed at a display on her left.

"What about those?" Stacie pointed at a rack of leather jackets to the right.

"Riding jackets. We can fit you with one of those, too, if you like. They're on sale," Carly said.

"Really?" Stacie looked at Donna and smiled.

Donna rolled her eyes. "Mom, you don't have to buy it just because it's on sale."

"No harm in looking, is there?" Stacie asked.

Thirty minutes later they walked out of Central Cycle and onto Bowness Road. Donna looked left and right at the renovated buildings and the new ones. She remembered that Bowness used to be its own town before being swallowed up by Calgary. She put the new helmet, still in its package, in the front corner of the pickup's box.

The inside of the cab smelled of leather. Donna grabbed her keys and looked right. Stacie lifted the collar of her new red leather jacket. She looked at Donna. "Thank you. Thank you very much."

Donna laughed, looked back at her mother, who lifted the left side of her lip, and laughed harder.

"Your laugh is beautiful." Stacie smiled as she worked her way out of the new leather. "I've always wanted a motorcycle jacket."

×

Matt lifted his vanilla latte and sipped its sweetness. He looked across the tiny table at his uncle—his mother's brother. *You have same eyes as my mother. You took me in when I arrived unexpectedly on your back doorstep with my clothes in a green garbage bag and my hockey equipment in another bag. Without asking any questions, you and Lane took me in.*

"Are we going to talk? We didn't say a word on the way home. And we didn't say a word in Co-Op when we dropped off Alexandre's prescriptions." Arthur put down his cup of tea.

Matt took a long breath and brushed at the front of his black T-shirt. "What do you want to know?"

"If you're okay. What the doctor said." Arthur's short, thick fingers played with the string on the tea bag.

"That's supposed to be confidential." Matt smiled.

"Sorry."

"I was joking, Uncle Arthur."

"Oh." Arthur made eye contact, then looked away.

"I told Alexandre about the nightmares, the trouble sleeping, and the loss of appetite. Then she asked me a series of questions." Matt fiddled with the lid on his paper cup.

Arthur looked over at the baristas who were chatting behind the cash register. The young woman had short-cut brunette hair and looked to be seven months pregnant. The young man had short sandy-blond hair and smiled as they talked.

"She told me that I had most of the symptoms of post-traumatic stress disorder. And she told me that ever since she had read about the kidnapping of Jessica and me, she'd been expecting a call from us. She said my symptoms are pretty typical after an experience like that. She said the medication should help with the anxiety and make it possible for me to sleep. She also thought that having the new puppy in the house might be a good thing." Matt reached for his cup. "What about you?"

"I asked her how come I felt so good after the operation— you know, so glad to be alive after the cancer diagnosis—and now I'm tired all the time." Arthur went back to fiddling with the string on his tea bag.

Matt took a sip of latte and waited.

"You know how you said I went from being a cancer survivor to being a cancer victim?"

Matt nodded.

"She said that the fatigue and the depression—her words, not mine—could be related and that I should take the medication, get more exercise, and get back to doing yoga. She said the physical activity would help."

"So, Uncle Lane was right about us needing to walk the dog." Matt shook his head.

"Just don't tell him that. He'll be insufferable." Arthur smiled.

"Still think he doesn't love you anymore?" Matt immediately regretted the question when his uncle began to cry.

×

Lori sat at her computer. Lane sat next to her in a chair he'd taken from the conference room.

She pointed at the screen. "This is what she sent to us using the parameters we provided."

"It's a long list. Is there any way we can put the various rentals on a map?" he asked.

"Give me a few minutes. I'll see what I can do." Lori reached for the phone.

Lane went into his office, picked up the phone, and entered the numbers for home. "Arthur?"

"We just got back," Arthur said.

"And?"

"Dr. Alexandre wants to see both of us again next week." Arthur said.

"And?"

"She thinks I'm depressed, so she gave me a prescription." *Cancer, the gift that keeps on giving.* "What about Matt?" Lane asked.

"We started to talk at Starbucks," Arthur said.

"And?"

"We decided that we need to take the dogs for more walks. And you and I need to get back to doing yoga."

"Yoga?" Lane thought. *Christ, not yoga again! Two gay guys doing downward dog in a room filled with women. We really are turning into stereotypes.*

"Yes."

There's something different in his tone of voice. "What's wrong?"

"You and I need to talk face to face about this. The phone is no good for what I need to say." Arthur hung up.

✕

Stacie opened her front door to a woman with short, wavy chestnut hair and wearing a navy-blue jacket and slacks. Next to her was a uniformed RCMP officer. Stacie felt fear rising in her throat as she remembered the last time a uniformed person had knocked at her front door to tell her what happened to Lisa. "Yes?"

"Stacie Laughton? I'm Keely Saliba, and I'm with the RCMP. May we come in?" Keely asked.

"What for?" Stacie put her fists on her hips.

"We'd like to discuss a recent purchase you made," Keely asked.

"I liked the leather jacket, so I bought it. What interest does the RCMP have in my jacket?" Stacie asked.

Keely closed her mouth and waited.

A few seconds later Stacie asked, "Would you like to come in?" She backed away from the front door.

Keely stepped inside, and the uniformed officer followed.

"You purchased a case of glycerine today." Keely studied Stacie's reaction.

Stacie's face turned red. "Yes."

"The reason for the purchase?" Keely asked.

"I'm a kindergarten teacher. I buy supplies for my classroom. It was on sale!" Stacie looked over her left shoulder.

Keely followed her gaze and saw the photograph of three people on the wall. A balding man stood between two younger women. One woman wore desert fatigues and a beret. Next to her, her twin wore jeans and a tank top. Both women smiled at the camera. "Your daughters?"

If it was possible to smile and frown at the same time, Stacie managed it. "Yes. Lisa and Donna. And their father."

"Twins?" Keely thought, *Why is this woman suddenly so sad?*

"Lisa was killed by a roadside bomb in Afghanistan. She was a medic. I thought that she would be safe because she was there to save lives. I was wrong." Stacie turned to face Keely.

Keely almost took a step back when she saw how the woman had aged in a sentence. Instead, she took a breath. "What do you use the glycerine for?"

Stacie looked Keely in the eye. "My husband died of a heart attack almost exactly one year to the day after Lisa was murdered by a bomber who hid and detonated the improvised explosive. A year after that, I was diagnosed with breast cancer. This family — what's left of my family — has earned the right to its privacy. I think I've answered enough questions for one day. Please leave."

Inside the unmarked RCMP cruiser, Keely reached for her laptop and asked the driver, "Is there a coffee shop nearby? I need wireless access. I've got some checking to do."

The driver asked, "Ever noticed how tiny women sometimes have the biggest balls?"

Keely smiled. "You talkin' 'bout me?"

The officer laughed. "Both you and Ms. Laughton, actually."

"Did you notice that she didn't answer the question when I asked her what she bought the glycerine for?"

×

"Make sure the butter goes right to the edge of the crust but no further." John A. Jones stood at his son's shoulder and watched to ensure that Chris made the sandwiches to exact specifications.

Chris thought, *Go fuck yourself.* "Mustard?"

"Yes, and spread the mustard just like the butter," John A. said.

"What time are we leaving in the morning?" Chris was careful to spread the condiments precisely.

"As soon as the west wind begins to pick up."

"Then we'd better start transferring the mix from the fridge into my pickup," Chris said.

"How long will it take?" John A. took the plate with the bread and began adding slices of ham.

Chris did a mental calculation. "At least four hours."

✕

Donna had just finished a small job and was hefting her tools into the back of her pickup when her phone rang. She lifted the air nailer onto the tailgate and reached into the chest pocket of her overalls. "Hello."

"The police came to see me!" Stacie said.

Oh, shit! Donna took a breath and looked around to see whether anyone on the construction site was near enough to overhear. "What did they want?"

"She was asking about the glycerine I bought," Stacie said.

"That was fast." *What's going on that I don't know about?*

"What do you want me to do?" Stacie asked.

"Have a cup of tea, have a nap, watch some daytime TV."

"What are you going to do?" Stacie asked.

"Get a cup of coffee and do some thinking. I'll call you back in a couple of hours." Donna hung up, checked to see that she'd put away all of her tools, and closed the tailgate.

✕

Christine sat at the kitchen table and cried.

Dan sat next to her, handed her tissue after tissue, and looked at Arthur.

Roz went to the door and whined to be let outside. Scout followed.

Arthur opened the back door and let the dogs out onto the deck. He closed the door and sat down across from them. "What happened?"

"She bought me makeup," Christine said.

Arthur looked at Dan, who seemed to be doing his best to shrink into his chair.

"Who bought you makeup?" Arthur asked.

"Lola." Christine pointed an accusatory finger at Dan. "His mother."

Daniel shrank some more.

"I'm not sure I understand," Arthur said.

"Christine and I were supposed to meet some of my mom's friends for supper at the golf club. My mom gave Christine some makeup to wear," Dan said.

"I still don't . . ." Arthur said.

Christine's eyes stopped her uncle mid-sentence. "It was a light base. She wanted me to wear it on my face, neck, and hands." Christine pointed to a lighter patch of skin on the back of her left hand. The skin was a light summer tan against Christine's cream-in-your-coffee skin. "She made an appointment with her hairdresser. She straightened my hair." Christine pulled at her black shoulder-length hair.

Arthur stared at Christine's hair and saw it had lost most of its natural curl. "*She* did that?" Arthur asked, then he glared at Daniel. "What the fuck is the matter with her?"

Daniel sat up straight in his chair. "We had a big fight. I'm moving out."

"There's more," Christine said.

Arthur looked at Christine. "What?"

"I'm pregnant."

"I thought you were on the pill." Arthur said.

"I was . . ." Christine began.

Arthur felt a smile spreading across his face. He could feel the familiar, almost forgotten thrill of joy rolling back in waves.

"Why are you smiling?" Daniel asked.

Christine began to cry again as she stood up. "I'm scared. I don't think I can be a good mother. And what if . . . what if Lola doesn't love the baby because it's black?"

Arthur's smile broadened as the words came to him. "Of course you'll be a good mother. And don't worry about Lola. Your baby will be perfect because its mother is perfect." He held out his arms.

Christine leaned into him. "Where's Matt?"

"Asleep." Arthur held her back with his right hand and pressed her closer. "You'll be fine." He saw Dan staring at the floor. "Daniel."

"What?" The young man lifted his head.

Arthur waved him over. He wrapped his arms around the pair and held them close. "We'll all be fine. The baby will be just fine."

×

Lane tucked his cell phone into his jacket pocket.

"What happened?" Lori sat at her computer. It was clicking and complaining away as it always did when it was doing a search. "You've gone white."

Nigel stepped through the office door and stopped.

"Ha. Funny. Lola bought Christine makeup to make *her* look white," Lane said.

"Bitch," Lori said.

"Who's Lola?" Nigel leaned on the counter.

"Dan's mother." Lane looked from Lori to Nigel.

"Who's Dan?" Nigel asked.

"Christine's boyfriend," Lane said.

"Who's Christine?" Nigel scratched his head with a paper clip.

Lori glared at Nigel, threw her arms up above her head, and smiled. "Enough with the questions."

"Christine is my niece. She's pregnant." *Why can't I keep my mouth shut? The words are just falling out like I have no control over what I say.* He looked at Nigel.

"Well?" Lori stared at Lane.

"Well, what?" Lane asked

Lori rolled her eyes. "Well, why are you here? Why aren't you on your way home?"

"We have a couple of guys who are about to set off a bomb," Lane said.

"In his neighbourhood." Nigel looked at Lori.

"So you need to go home, see Christine, and be closer to the suspects when we find their exact location." Lori pointed at herself and then at Nigel.

"We'll be in constant contact with you when it comes to any and all new information," Nigel said.

"Let's just assume that the Jones boys aren't —" Lori looked at Nigel and mimed throwing a football.

"— living next door to you." Nigel pretended to catch the ball and winked at Lori.

×

Donna poured the last of the glycerine into the funnel set into the seventy-five–litre container in the back of the van.

She checked the time on her cell phone and began adding the second chemical. Her shoulders and back ached from being bent over in the cramped quarters in the back of the van. She looked left at the metal wall of the panel van and thought, *The last thing Lisa saw was the metal walls of an armoured personnel carrier.*

She used both hands to empty the four-litre container into the funnel. *Once this is done, both vans will be ready. Then I'll test to make sure everything is working the way it should.*

✕

Lane opened the front door of his house and listened for any clues that would prepare him for whatever was going on inside.

Roz ran up the stairs from the family room to see who had arrived. She wagged her tail and approached him, expecting a scratch.

Lane rubbed the dog under her chin. Scout was next to work his way up the stairs. When his tail wagged, his entire body wiggled. Lane rubbed him under the chin too.

Lane kicked off his shoes and followed the sound of conversation down the stairs and into the family room.

Christine sat next to Dan on the couch. Arthur sat in the leather easy chair. Matt sat next to him in the rocker. Next-door neighbour Maria had her legs tucked under her in the leather tub chair.

Lane looked at Christine and Dan. Conversation stopped. Eyes turned to Lane. *Just say what you've practised all the way here.* "I hear congratulations are in order."

Christine smiled, stood, and hugged Lane around the neck. "Are you mad at me?"

"No. I'm just happy." Lane could feel her tears on the side of his neck.

"Are you mad at me?" Dan stood with his legs shoulder-width apart, one leg set slightly back.

Once again all eyes were focused on Lane, who walked over to Dan and shook his hand.

"Have some pizza." Matt took a hefty bite out of a slice.

He turned to Christine. "We haven't seen much of you lately. Does this mean we'll be seeing you more often?"

Christine blushed. "I was trying to get to know Dan's parents. When we found out I was pregnant, well, we thought . . ." She looked to Dan.

"We thought that, you know, it would be better if my parents knew Christine better before we told them." Dan looked around the room gauging everyone's reactions. He avoided eye contact with Lane.

"We all know how well that worked out." Matt chewed as he spat out the words.

Christine said, "This isn't a joke!"

"Yes, but you do deserve a little bit of a hard time. We —" Matt pointed at Lane and Arthur "— felt you'd moved on to bigger and better things."

Daniel shook his head. "It wasn't like that."

Lane looked at Dan, who continued to avoid eye contact. "Dan?" Lane asked.

Dan stood up and took a long breath.

He's still expecting me to be mad at him, Lane thought before he stood and opened his arms to hug Dan.

"I love her," Dan said just loud enough for Lane to hear.

"How come you came home, Uncle Lane? I thought you were after some crazy bomber guy," Matt said.

Lane looked at his nephew, who was licking his fingers after devouring another wedge of pizza. "Good to see you've got your appetite back. The pizza parlours can expect larger profits next week."

"Bomber?" Maria instinctively put her hand on her belly as if to ward off any danger to the baby.

"Some guy is getting together the chemicals to make a bomb, and Uncle Lane is looking for him." Matt waved at the air between him and Maria. "When my uncle is on the trail, the bad guys are out of luck."

"Want some pizza?" Christine put a slice on a plate and handed it to Lane.

He took the plate and sat down on the couch. "Good idea. Then I'm just going to close my eyes for a minute."

Maria asked, "Does this have anything to do with that Poulin woman?"

×

Chris removed his PVC gloves. His hands were slippery with sweat. He reached up to remove the mask from his face. He looked at the sealed stainless-steel containers in rows and recessed into the metal framework Oscar Mendes had welded. Chris closed the lid of the metal drum bolted onto a base in the bed of his Chevy pickup. The round container behind the cab looked like a red diesel fuel tank complete with filler pipe. He was struck by a flashback of Oscar welding the tank and the searing white-hot burn of the welder as molten metal sealed the sections together.

"That's the last of it?" his father asked.

Chris nodded. "Now we need to hook up the refrigeration unit."

"What for?" John A. glared at his son.

Chris stared at the empty containers in the fridges with their doors open and their lights on. "The mixture becomes unstable as it warms."

"Have faith. The outside air is cool, and we'll leave early in the morning. The west winds are forecast to be at twenty kilometres per hour by then. I'll drive your truck. You follow in mine. By lunchtime we'll be in Edmonton. By supper time we'll be home."

Chris shook his head. "It's not about faith; it's about science. Eight degrees centigrade is where this stuff is most stable."

John A. dismissed his son with a wave. "We'll see if your science wins over my faith."

Your faith didn't win over my mother's cancer. Chris stared at the connection that would hook the refrigeration unit in the tank to the auxiliary battery under the hood of the Chevy.

✕

Donna parked the grey van next to the white one in the middle of a lot bordered by shops, restaurants, and movie theatres.

She locked the van door and began the walk back to her house. As she walked, she ticked off a mental list of things she'd already done to ensure that nothing had been forgotten.

Fifteen minutes later, she walked up to her house. Her truck was parked out front, and the Harley was strapped on its trailer attached to the rear of the truck.

She took a look around. All of the vehicles on the street were familiar. She walked up to the driver's door of her pickup, opened it, climbed in, started the truck, and drove away. On the seat beside her were her sleeping bag, two helmets, a thermos of coffee, a pillow, and the desert camouflage jacket Lisa had given her the day she left for Afghanistan.

chapter 10

Weatherman Helps with Stampede Record

Eight days of warm, dry, sunny weather have helped push this year's Stampede attendance beyond even the most ambitious predictions.

Friday is expected to be another record breaker even though temperatures are forecast to be somewhat cooler.

If past years are any indication, the last Friday of Stampede draws the largest crowds. It is expected that the grandstand will be filled to capacity for the rodeo finals tonight.

The finals of the chuckwagon and bronc-riding events usually bring the biggest crowds. At this pace, total attendance may reach 1.5 million, beating all previous records.

Lane sat up on the couch.

Matt was screaming.

Lane stood. The white comforter someone had covered him with fell to the floor. He looked at his plate on the coffee table. His pizza was gone. Roz looked up at him with guilty brown eyes. Scout licked his lips, stretched his front legs, and did his version of downward dog. *How long have I been asleep?*

He walked over to Matt's bedroom door and knocked. "Matt?"

Matt said, "He killed her!"

Shit. Lane knocked on the door. "Matt!"

Silence.

"What?" Matt's voice was distorted by phlegm and fear.

"You're having a nightmare."

The sound of footsteps. The door opened. Matt's eyes were wild.

"You okay?" *Stupid question!*

Matt looked at the floor. "I felt so good yesterday."

"Want me to make some coffee?" *This is going to be a long haul, Matt.*

"Sure." Matt closed his door.

Lane went upstairs, started the water boiling, and ground some beans for the Bodum.

His phone rang and he reached for it. "Lane here."

"Things are happening. We're at the Starbucks across from the Co-Op. You are needed," Keely said.

"On my way." Lane pressed the end button on his phone.

Matt stepped into the kitchen wearing his work clothes and saw the expression on his uncle's face. "Gotta go?"

Lane nodded. "I'm sorry, Matt. You wouldn't be going through this if it weren't for . . ."

"For what?" Matt put his hand on Lane's shoulder. "I'd be on the street if it weren't for you and Arthur."

Lane saw the clarity in Matt's eyes. "Just pour the water in after it boils and let it sit for four minutes."

Matt nodded. "See you later."

Ten minutes later, Lane spotted Keely and Nigel in a black, unmarked four-door pickup truck. Keely lifted a coffee. Lane parked next to the truck and climbed in the back seat.

Keely handed him a cup. "Extra-hot mochaccino."

"How come you didn't call me last night?" Lane asked.

"Lori said one of us needed to be clear headed this morning." Nigel turned around in his seat to face Lane. "We need to get you up to speed."

Keely gripped the steering wheel and pointed at the red-and-white flag waving over the building supply store. "The wind is blowing from the west. The evidence Nigel has gathered suggests that Jones wants to give a major city a taste of what the rural areas endure with oil companies."

"Remember how Jones said that the people in the cities wouldn't understand what the pollution was like until it happened to them?" Nigel asked.

Lane nodded as he took a sip of coffee.

Keely handed him a breakfast sandwich. She pointed at a grey unmarked Chev. "That's your car."

"Thanks." Lane unwrapped the sandwich, took a bite, and chased it with coffee.

"We've narrowed Jones's location down to three possible houses. All have double garages. All ordered groceries from over there." Nigel pointed at the Co-Op across the street. The white-tipped mountains were just visible over the roof of the Co-Op.

"And?" Lane asked.

"We're waiting. If we're right about the amount of explosive, then we need to sit back until Jones makes his move. The collateral damage from an explosion like that . . ." Keely shrugged instead of finishing the sentence.

Nigel tapped his handheld computer. "The most likely target is the extraction plant on the west side of the city. The plant extracts and stores natural gas and a variety of liquids. All are flammable. One is heavier than air and will cause asphyxiation. It will settle into hollows. The forecast is for winds of thirty kilometres an hour, which would push the cloud of gas into residential areas, including this one." He handed the computer to Lane.

Lane looked at a map of the city. Nigel had used purple to shade the northwestern quadrant of the city. "What kind of perimeter have you set up?"

"All exits to Ranchlands are being monitored. That includes the buses-only underpass into Dalhousie. Fire and ambulance have been alerted. HAWCS is standing by." Keely set her coffee in a cup holder in the centre console.

Nigel said, "The plan is to tail him until he's out of the city, stop him on the highway before he reaches the extraction plant, arrest him, or — worst case — detonate the bomb where there will be the least amount of collateral damage."

Keely said, "The RCMP is blocking the entrance to the extraction plant and extra cruisers are waiting along major routes out of the city in case we're wrong and Jones takes another route."

"Sounds like you've got it covered," Lane said.

"If we're right and he's been waiting for the optimum weather conditions, then it looks like this is it." Nigel pointed at the rippling flag.

"What are you not telling me?" Lane asked.

Nigel looked at Keely.

Keely took a long breath. "We have another suspect. She used her charge card to purchase a case of glycerine. I interviewed her. She's hiding something. And she has a motive."

"Name?" Lane shoved the last piece of breakfast sandwich into his mouth.

Keely said, "Stacie Laughton. Daughter was a medic in Afghanistan who was killed by a roadside bomb. Stacie lost her husband a year later. She says she bought the glycerine for her kindergarten class, but she was evasive and something doesn't add up."

Lane looked out the windshield at the grey tips of the mountains. "Does Laughton have another daughter?"

"Yes, a twin to the medic. I checked on her as well. She's a contractor. Lives on her own. Divorced. Has a restraining order out on an abusive husband. Nigel found out a bit more."

Nigel reached over the seat and tapped an icon on his computer. A video played. It showed a rally in downtown Calgary in front of the federal building. The brownstone-and-glass structure was in the background. Stacie and Donna Laughton were in the foreground. Donna was holding a sign. WARS BEGIN WITH WORDS. Her mother held another sign. TALK PEACE.

Lane looked closely at the image. "I've met her."

"And?" Keely asked.

"I was walking the dog and saw her stop two guys from stealing from a neighbour's house," Lane said.

"And?" Keely stared at him.

"We sat down for a beer."

"Do you think she's planning something?" Nigel asked.

Lane thought back and remembered the rusted van parked out front. "What does the evidence say?"

"We can't find a connection between the Laughtons and Jones," Nigel said.

"And I'm sure the mother is withholding information," Keely said.

"Who is our primary focus then?" Lane asked.

"Jones." Nigel looked at Keely.

"I agree, but we can't afford to ignore this other evidence," Keely said.

"Donna Laughton has a van parked in front of her house. It had something painted on the side." Lane closed his eyes as he visualized the van.

"We went to her house. There was no one home and no van parked out front." Keely looked directly at Lane. "What was this Donna like?"

"She didn't seem to be afraid of taking on the two thieves," Lane said.

"I don't want to dismiss the possibility of a coordinated strike. If we're looking for one explosive device and end up with two, the likelihood of fatalities increases exponentially." Keely opened her hands with the palms up.

The implication for Nigel and Lane was clear. None of them wanted blood on their hands.

Keely said, "Nigel and I will keep one eye on the Laughton angle." She pointed at Lane. "Jones is the one with the motive and the means to carry this out. You concentrate on him."

$\times$

"I'll drive your truck, and you follow with mine." John A. Jones grabbed the bag of sandwiches and handed it to Chris. "Take these with you."

"There's one problem. How will you detonate?" Chris asked.

John A. tapped the side of his head with a forefinger. "There are blasting caps in my truck. I've been saving them for this."

Chris handed his keys to his father. "Did you switch on the refrigeration unit?"

"Get me the blasting caps and quit worrying. I've done this before. All you need to do is follow my lead."

Chris thought, *It was cool last night. Got down around ten degrees centigrade. Maybe it'll be okay.*

$\times$

Lane's phone rang. He looked at Keely and Nigel before he brought the phone to his ear. "Lane."

"It's Cam."

He sounds calm. He gets like this when something big is about to happen.

"Are you up to speed?" Harper asked.

"Yes." Lane looked at the words of wisdom on the side of his coffee cup.

"You concentrate on the primary target. You've got the lead. We've got all other major routes covered in case he heads for downtown or a target we haven't considered. The interception points are located where the least amount of damage will occur if he detonates." Harper waited.

"Why are you telling me this?" Lane looked out the windshield as a line of cars waited for the light to turn green.

"I want your mind cleared of all other distractions. We're covered. Now you just do your job."

"And?" Lane asked.

"And I'll talk with you when it's all over." Harper hung up.

×

Donna's phone rang as she sat drinking her coffee at the local Starbucks. She lifted her phone out of her bib pocket, looked at the number, felt her chest tighten, and lifted the phone to her ear. "Hi, Sue."

"Is this a good time to talk?"

"It's good." Donna looked at the coffee in her left hand and set down her half-finished bacon-and-egg sandwich with her right.

"Del and I have been talking things over," Sue said.

"And?" Donna put her coffee down next to the half-eaten sandwich. Anxiety made it impossible to swallow.

"I have some questions."

Donna heard the tension in Sue's voice. "Go ahead."

"Are you in love with my husband?" Sue asked.

"No."

There was a pause at the other end. "Then why him?"

"He's the best man I know," Donna said.

"Oh."

Donna waited.

"Then the next thing we need to talk about is that Del just can't walk away if you go ahead with it. And I can't either."

"What would you like to do?" Donna looked up as a woman calmed an angry toddler who was trying to climb out of a stroller.

"We would like to make a deal with you. An arrangement. Argh! Do you find that there aren't any words that help you to say what you mean in a situation like this?"

✕

Chris followed his father over the bridge on Crowchild Trail. He looked right at the traffic coming down Stoney Trail. It travelled underneath the bridge and made its way down to the Bow River valley. He looked ahead. Waves of heat rose from the pavement. He looked at the cab of his white, black, and red truck and saw his father's shoulders and head. Chris had salvaged the Chevy from the parts of three cannibalized trucks. He saw heat distorting the air above the cab.

Chris grabbed his cell phone and dialed. He watched as his father reached for the phone on the seat beside him and brought it to his ear. "Yep."

"Dad. Remember that the stuff gets unstable as its temperature rises. Stay away from any bumps in the road."

"I told you not to worry. There's a gap between what faith can accomplish and what science is able to explain. My faith will carry us through." John A. Jones hung up.

Chris put the phone into the cup holder between the seats of his father's truck. He looked ahead and saw that they would soon be out of the city. He looked at the mountains. Their white tips and grey shoulders seemed so close — an illusion created by atmospheric conditions.

×

Lane's phone rang and vibrated. He held it up to his ear. "Lane here."

Harper said, "The suspect vehicle is on the move. It's headed west on Crowchild Trail just as your team predicted. Units from other locales are converging on the scene to help block traffic. HAWCS says she can pick you up at the soccer field in Ranchlands. Are you able?"

"On my way." Lane hung up, started the engine, and hit the lights.

One minute later, he parked on the upper edge of the playing fields with their panoramic perspective of downtown high-rises that rose out of the river valley fifteen kilometres away. Lane watched the helicopter hover and then land at the centre of the field about fifty metres from the playground. Lane shut and locked the door of his car, then ran down the hill and onto the flat. The grass was spongy under his feet. He crouched as he came within range of the helicopter's rotor. The disturbed air and the jet engine created its own chaotic environment of kerosene fumes and dancing debris from the fresh-cut grass. Lane stepped on the footpad on the strut, opened the door, and climbed inside.

The pilot — the name *Lacey* was on her blue flight suit — wore a helmet. She watched as he climbed in and put on the safety harness. She pointed at a headset.

Lane put on the headset and adjusted the mic. "Let's go." He felt the helicopter lift and watched the field shrink beneath his feet. The pilot swung the tail around. The city centre was behind them and the mountains were out front. Lane looked down. An adult led a line of toddlers climbing the path to the playground. He could see that each child held onto a rope. For a moment, he saw their faces as they looked up at the helicopter. One waved at him. Lane waved back.

The helicopter accelerated. The pilot said, "Roads are being blocked behind the suspect vehicle. We should have a visual in two or three minutes."

Lane looked ahead. Crowchild Trail crossed over Stoney Trail. The western edge of the city was a road marked with houses and condos on one side and acreages and golf courses on the other. To the south, the Bearspaw Reservoir was like the head of the Bow River snake winding its way back to the Rocky Mountains.

To the northwest he could make out the stacks of the extraction plant.

"We have a visual on the vehicle," Lacey said.

Lane looked at the four-lane highway. Traffic was stopped at the lights marking access to Bearspaw School on one side of the highway and Bearspaw Community Hall on the other. A red truck was fourth in a row of vehicles in the right lane. Ahead of it was a white, black, and red truck with an auxiliary fuel tank set in the front of the box.

Lane looked down and to his right. He could see police cruisers — out of sight of the red pickup because they were hidden by the crest of a hill — stopping the flow of traffic behind the trucks.

The light turned green.

The vehicles at the lights began to accelerate. They travelled about one hundred metres down the highway.

An unmarked car pulled in front of the red truck. Another pulled up beside the suspect vehicle. A third pulled up behind the truck. Lane watched as the four vehicles pulled over to the shoulder, doors opened, and officers pointed their weapons at the driver.

Lacey set the helicopter into hover. A gust of wind made the helicopter buck.

Lane felt a rush of nausea. He looked farther down the highway at the multicoloured pickup. Black smoke poured from its exhaust. He pointed at the escaping vehicle. "We need to follow the white-and-black truck with the fuel tank in the rear."

Lacey nodded. "The one that's passing in the left lane?"

"Correct. We also need to alert the officers at the extraction plant that the truck is en route. How do I connect with Chief Simpson?" Lane asked.

Lacey tapped a communications switch with her thumb as she aimed HAWCS west to pursue the fleeing pickup.

"Hello?" Lane asked.

"What's the situation?" Simpson asked.

"One suspect vehicle has been stopped. We are in pursuit of what I believe is the primary target with the explosives."

"You are aware that deadly force is authorized for our officers and the RCMP officers on scene?" Simpson asked.

"I am. Is approaching traffic being shut down?"

"Already done," Simpson said.

"We will stop the bomber."

"Let me be clear. I want there to be no civilian casualties and no police casualties," Simpson said.

"Understood." Lane pointed at Lacey and tapped the side of his headset. He saw her flick the communications switch. "How close can we get?"

Lacey adjusted the controls, and they began to descend.

Lane looked to his left. The extraction plant, with its silver stacks, towers, and storage tanks, was about five kilometres away. He saw the access road about half a kilometre down the highway. He pointed at the plant. "He'll turn right up there. We need to set down on the road about a kilometre this side of the plant. Land on the road to block his access. Then we'll wait until the officers in the marked units catch up."

He looked down at the road and saw where the pavement ended and the gravel began. He could see how the passage of heavy vehicles had created hollows in the wavy washboard surface of the gravel road.

Lacey set the helicopter down on a patch of paved road about five hundred metres from the extraction plant. "Do you want me inside or out?" she asked.

"We need both weapons," Lane said.

Lacey began to work on the shutdown checklist.

Lane hung up his headset and undid his harness. When the rotor slowed, he stepped outside and walked to the ditch. He looked back at the helicopter as the individual blades of the rotor became discernable.

Lacey appeared around the nose of the helicopter and nodded at Lane. Her brown hair was stuck to her skull. She'd left her helmet inside the chopper.

Lane pointed at the ditch opposite to his.

The rotor stopped. Its mechanical sounds were replaced by the wind and the distant rumble of an approaching vehicle.

The multicoloured pickup accelerated up the hill below them. Jones was less than a kilometre away.

Lane pulled his Glock from its holster. He looked over his shoulder at the extraction plant and knew there would be a team of officers readying their weapons. If Jones got past Lane and Lacey, they would be the final line of defense.

Lane looked along the east side of the road where green grain waved and bent in the wind. He looked to the west side and nodded at Lacey. He saw that she had her Glock ready. Lane looked down the hill. The truck approached the stretch of gravel. He looked down and slid a round into the Glock's chamber. *He'll have to be very close before we'll be able to open fire.*

The truck hit the edge of the gravel road. Jones was about three hundred metres away and closing. A plume of dust rose up behind the rear wheels of the truck. Headlights flanked the open maw that was once the pickup's grille. Lane could see the driver behind the steering wheel.

Lane watched the rear of the truck buck as it hit a hump in the washboard. It bounced once. The driver corrected as the rear end swung east.

The back wheels of the truck hit a hole.

The tail end of the truck bounced a second time. This time the wheels appeared to come off the ground.

The wheels touched, and the truck bottomed out. The tires on the front end splayed out.

A flash of light silhouetted the driver hunched over the wheel. The truck evaporated in a blast of light and dust.

Debris shot though the sand-coloured cloud. Lane blinked and stepped back. He watched the wave of the aftershock tsunami its way through the green wheat. The sound of the blast reached them.

He felt the concussion in his chest. It forced him back two more steps.

A tire dropped out of the sky, bounced on the road, wobbled, rolled into the ditch, and fell on its side.

The roof of the truck floated down, slipped sideways, then began to spin leaf-like to the ground.

Lane looked at Lacey.

"What the hell happened?" she asked.

Lane's phone rang. He ejected the clip from his Glock, then the round, and put the clip and bullet in his jacket pocket before tucking the gun into its holster. He reached for the phone. "Lane."

"We may be in the middle of a coordinated attack," Keely said.

"Explain." Lane breathed deeply to calm his nerves.

"A van is parked in the lot behind Eagle's Nest Christian Church. The church has its Stampede breakfast this morning. The minister phoned to report an abandoned vehicle. He thinks it might be loaded with explosives in reaction to their Quran incident," Keely said.

Lane thought for a moment. "Anything painted on the side of the van?"

"Beauty could use a little help to save the world," Keely said.

"Just to be safe, follow procedure. Cordon the lot off. Evacuate the church. We'll be there in a few minutes." Lane waved at Lacey and pointed to the chopper. She nodded, climbed inside, and put her helmet on.

Lane grabbed the handle attached to the helicopter's metal frame, climbed in, then got himself belted and hooked in. *Keep your mind clear, think slowly, forget about Jones, and concentrate on this new situation.*

"What about the scene?" Lacey pointed at the cloud of smoke and dust that drifted east with the wind.

By now they'll have heard about or seen the explosion. Many people at the church will be close to panic. "Alert forensics and request that the marked units cordon off the scene until after the bomb squad clears the area. Right now we have a more pressing situation."

Lacey nodded as she began the start-up procedures.

After they lifted off, Lacey flew over the scene of the explosion. Lane looked down. The crater in the road stretched from ditch to ditch. Next to the crater was part of the truck's frame. The engine was in the ditch. A shred of clothing stuck to the barbwire fence. It flapped in the wind. Lane saw the truck's steering wheel this side of the crater. A hand still gripped the wheel. The arm attached to the hand ended at the elbow.

Lacey looked east. He heard his headphones crackle.

"What the hell happened?" Harper demanded.

Lane shook the image of the severed arm out of his mind. "Jones blew himself up. I can't talk right now. I need to think ahead. There's another situation."

Within four minutes, they hovered over the church parking lot. Lacey was careful to stay wide of the power lines and the nearby power station.

Lane took in the scene as they hovered. Black-and-white police cars had the entrance to the church parking lot blocked off. The van was parked at the north end of the lot. At the south end stood a line of tables with red-and-white-checked tablecloths flapping in the wind and portable griddles for making pancakes. *Go with the evidence, then go with your gut. A connection between Jones and Donna doesn't add up. Don't listen to the fear. Think this through!*

✕

Donna found her mother in the parking lot where she'd left both vans. The second van was parked exactly where Donna had left it the night before. She pulled up on the driver's side, shut off her Harley, leaned it onto its kickstand, and took off her sunglasses. There was a sweet, heavy stink of gasoline in the air.

Stacie rolled down the driver's side window of the van. "It won't start."

"It's probably flooded," Donna said.

"How do you know that?" Stacie looked at her daughter like she had either caught her in a lie or just made the discovery that Donna was a psychic.

"Take your right foot, put it on the gas pedal, and press it halfway to the floor." Donna leaned against the door.

"Okay." Stacie stepped on the gas pedal.

"Turn the key." Donna tapped her upper lip with a forefinger.

The starter whined. The engine coughed, then caught.

White smoked pooped from the exhaust pipe.

"I'll follow you to the Islamic Centre." Donna put her sunglasses on, straddled her bike, leaned it upright, and hit the starter.

×

Chris leaned forward. His hands were cuffed behind his back. He was in the rear seat of a police cruiser as it travelled east along Crowchild Trail toward the centre of the city.

The officer who sat next to the driver turned to Chris. "You doin' okay back there?"

Chris nodded and smiled. His smile turned into a grin.

"Wanna share the joke?" the officer asked.

Chris thought for a moment. "I'm free."

The officer laughed — a sharp, short bark — and said, "You're kidding, right?"

Chris shook his head. "Nope."

×

Lane closed the helicopter door, stepped away from the machine, waved at Lacey, then turned and walked downhill over the uneven ground of the vacant lot toward the Eagle's Nest Christian Church, which looked down at John Laurie Boulevard and a daycare. It was in the final stages of being evacuated. Toddlers were being loaded onto a city bus.

He felt the blast of wind from the rotors as the helicopter lifted off. He put his hand over his eyes as dust whirled around him. *I'll need a shower after this*, he thought, tasted grit on his tongue, and went to spit. *Not yet! You'll wear it!*

The wind subsided, quickly replaced by a gusty thirty-kilometre-per-hour wind from the west.

He looked toward the church, turned his head, and spat. Keely waved from outside of the barricade. He walked toward her. *Just keep your cool.* His body shivered as he flashed back to the shock of the explosion and the image of Jones's arm still attached to the steering wheel.

When he got closer, Keely asked, "How far away were you from the blast?"

"Maybe two hundred metres." Lane looked at the van parked next to a retaining wall in the church parking lot. The church was a sand-coloured stucco structure. "What's the news on the van?" Lane asked.

"We've got an ID for the owner. It's Donna Laughton, the daughter of the woman I talked to about the glycerine," Keely said.

"The bomb disposal unit is on its way." Nigel looked west and shook his head as he watched the approaching dust cloud reaching five hundred metres into the sky, an ominous reminder of what Jones intended to do.

"The only person harmed so far was the driver of the truck. Let's keep it that way." Lane heard a noise and looked at the street running along the west side of the church.

×

Donna's Harley idled at the lights at John Laurie Boulevard. She looked to her left and saw the cream-coloured stucco of Eagle's Nest Church.

"How come we didn't start up the van when we dropped it off?" Stacie wore her new helmet and red leather jacket. She perched on the rear seat with her arms wrapped around her daughter.

"It takes a few minutes for the mixture to settle. That's why I had to get remote starters for both. And Mom?" Donna asked.

"What?"

"Can you get your hands off my boobs?"

"Oh, sorry." Stacie lowered her hands, then held on tight

to Donna's waist when the light turned green and Donna opened the throttle.

"So, you think this will be easy?" Lisa, the dead sister voice in Donna's head, asked.

Donna shifted into second, leaned left into the turn, and wondered why Lisa had decided to talk with her at this moment. "Where have you been?"

"Keeping an eye on you and Mom. Never thought I'd see Mom on the back of your motorcycle."

"I think the red leather jacket fulfills one of her secret fantasies." Donna looked up the hill.

"I hope you two aren't doing this just because of me. That would be such a dramatic gesture. It's not like you at all," Lisa said.

"You know why I'm doing this." Donna spotted a black-and-white police cruiser parked across the entrance to the church parking lot. Then she saw the yellow tape marking the perimeter. *Shit, I have to stop to get the remote out of my pocket.* She pulled over to the curb, squeezed the clutch, and stopped. She put her right foot on the curb to steady the bike. Her leg strained at the combined weight of the bike and her mother. "Mom, help me out here. Put your foot on the curb."

"Why?" Stacie asked before doing as she was told.

Donna took a moment to look at the two men and one woman standing next to the car. She recognized one of the men as she reached into her pocket, pulled out the remote starter, pointed it at the van, and pressed the button.

Lane raised his arm to stop her. "Hey!"

Donna watched the van and saw a blue puff of exhaust billow from its tail pipe. She stuffed the remote back in her pocket, opened the throttle, eased out the clutch. The bike stalled. "Shit!" She realized too late that she'd left the bike in second gear. She pulled back the clutch, took the weight of the bike on her left leg, shifted into first with her right, and hit the starter.

She could see her neighbour — the detective — in her rear-view mirror. He ran and pointed at her. "Stop!"

A younger cop reached for his weapon.

A young woman ran past Detective Lane.

The Harley's engine roared. Donna opened the throttle a touch, eased out the clutch, and pulled away. Stacie almost squeezed the air out of her lungs.

Lane stopped, turned, and ran for the car. He pointed at Nigel, then at the unmarked car. "Start it up!" He looked at Keely and — with an apology implied, knowing he was choosing between two partners — asked, "Can you stay here?"

Keely frowned and nodded.

Lane pointed at the parked vehicles across the street. "Get behind one of those cars just in case." Lane climbed into the passenger seat as Nigel started the engine.

The tires chirped, then Nigel accelerated up the hill. "I've called for black-and-whites to block the exits."

Lane nodded as he did up his seat belt.

Ahead, the passenger wearing the red leather jacket on the back of the Harley looked over her shoulder.

Stacie said, "The police are following us. Their lights are flashing."

"I know, Mom. We just have to get back down the hill to start up the other van. Then we'll stop." Donna down shifted and turned the corner.

"It looks like they're not going to pull over." Nigel closed on the Harley as he turned on the siren.

A police car approached from the east. The driver turned across two lanes.

Donna downshifted, turned right, travelled down a paved alley, bumped over a curb, and bounced over a stretch of grass running between two fences. "Hold on, Mom."

Donna eased the bike over the crest of a hill and down onto the flat of a baseball diamond.

"Want me to follow?" Nigel asked.

Lane shook his head. "No, just take a right up there by the gas station. She'll probably end up back on the road."

"You sure?" Nigel asked.

Lane nodded. "I sometimes walk the dogs up here."

Nigel turned the corner and accelerated.

Donna pointed the bike down another hill, then along the flat, and headed for a gap in the trees near the sidewalk.

Lisa said, "Look, sis, you've proved you know how to ride a bike. Pull over before this gets out of hand."

"I just need to start up the second van. Then I'll stop and talk." Donna reached the sidewalk, bumped over the curb, turned right down the hill, opened the throttle, shifted into a higher gear, and headed for John Laurie Boulevard.

"There's nothing to prove," Lisa said.

The Harley's engine roared. Ahead, the light was red. Donna looked in her mirror. The unmarked police car was closing. She shifted down a gear, thinking she might need the acceleration. "Hold on tight, Mom."

Lisa said, "Believe me, this little adventure of yours could turn deadly any second now."

"Remember? You didn't listen to me when I told you not to go to Afghanistan," Donna said.

"So this is what it's all about. You're still mad at me?" Lisa asked.

Lane's phone rang as Nigel closed to within ten metres of the motorcycle.

Lane looked at the face of his phone, recognized the number, and answered, "Lane." He listened, then said, "You can't be serious!"

Nigel said, "I think she's going to run the red light."

Lane pressed the phone's end button. "Turn your siren off!"

"What?" Nigel asked.

"Do it!"

Nigel shut the siren off.

"Now pull up beside her so the traffic on John Laurie can see our lights if she decides to run the red," Lane said.

"This is crazy!" Nigel pulled into the left-hand lane and accelerated, then braked to match the speed of the bike.

"That's it! Perfect!" Lane looked to his right.

Donna looked down at him.

Lane smiled, raised his hands, turned them palms down, pushed them downward, and mouthed the words *Slow it down*.

Donna nodded at Lane, braked, looked right and left, and then shot through a gap in the westbound traffic.

A driver approaching from the east saw the police car's lights and braked.

Donna made it through the intersection.

"Great work, Nigel! Now follow her. I'll call off the marked units before someone gets hurt."

Donna saw a police car approaching with its lights flashing and its siren howling. Then it slowed, its lights went off, and the siren stopped.

Donna turned right at the intersection, drove halfway down the block, and pulled into the parking lot between the Islamic Centre and the local watering hole. She shut off the bike, waited for her mother to climb off the back, leaned the Harley onto its kickstand, and reached into her left pocket. She pulled out the second remote, pointed it at the grey van, and pressed the button. The engine started.

Out of the corner of her eye, Donna spotted a quartet of boys who looked to be fifteen or sixteen bounding out of the Islamic Centre. One of the boys held up a book. He moved to the middle of the parking lot and began to dance in a circle as he held the book aloft. The other three stood around the boy with the book and clapped their hands.

Stacie took her helmet off, rubbed some life back into her hair, and checked her look in the mirror. "Is it going to work?"

"It takes a minute." Donna watched the boys as the one in the centre opened the book, tore out a page, and pantomimed wiping his ass.

"Is that a Bible?" Stacie asked.

"I think so."

More people were spilling out of the Islamic Centre. They stopped to watch the boys.

The boy in the middle held the book out for the other three. All tore out pages and began to dance around, pretending to wipe their backsides with the gospel.

Lane walked up beside Donna. "How are you today?"

Donna looked at him and smirked. "Busted." She turned and watched as the first bubble formed and detached itself from the roof of the van.

"Did you know about the bomb?" Lane asked.

"Bomb?" Donna turned back to face the detective.

"Harrah!" a woman shouted as she emerged from the Islamic Centre.

Nigel, Lane, Donna, and Stacie all looked at the tableau of capering boys and gathering crowd with their flowing clothing billowing in the wind.

One woman was a little over five feet tall. She wore a red hijab and a long black outfit that almost covered the toes of her black shoes. She raised her arms. "Haven't you learned anything? Mohammed walked under the window of that woman who threw filth down on him. He never fought back, and then when she was ill, he nursed her back to health. This is not how you are taught to act!"

The boys stopped.

"Fatima! Let the boys alone! They are only doing what that Poulin woman did to the Quran!" A man in a black suit stood just outside the door of the Islamic Centre.

Fatima shook her head. "No! This is Canada. I do not have to be quiet! You be quiet, Ahmed! You and your friend Shefic think that it's honourable to kill a child and a grandchild! You brought dishonour on all of us!" She pointed her index finger at the man for effect, then opened her hand and wiped the air in front of her face in an act of dismissal.

A bubble of soap floated over her head.

Ahmed looked around him for support. No one looked his way.

Children pushed their way out from the crowd. One popped a floating bubble. Other children joined in and began to chase the bubbles. Squeals of joy followed the sound of children's laughter. The laughter spread as the cloud of bubbles thickened and swirled.

Donna turned to Lane. "Can you let us enjoy this for a minute or two?" She put her arm around her mother's shoulder. "My sister would have liked this."

Lane saw tears running down Stacie's cheeks. She leaned into her daughter's embrace. He turned to watch as the boys handed over the pages torn from the Bible. Fatima gathered the pages and stuck them back inside the book. Around her, the younger children danced, laughed, and chased bubbles.

The wind shifted. The bubbles turned back on themselves and gathered on the leeward side of the Islamic Centre.

A cloud of dust from Jones's explosion passed over them. The filtered sunlight created a series of rainbows in the soap bubbles that swirled skyward in a column of colour.

"Absofuckinlutely beautiful," Nigel said.

Fatima tucked the book under her arm. She walked away from the crowd and stopped. Two young boys, a daughter, and her husband joined her. The boys, the daughter, and the father all stood between Fatima and the crowd. The daughter stepped back and put her arm around her mother's shoulder. They looked at the bands of orange, yellow, and blue momentarily suspended in the air.

More children spilled out of the Islamic Centre as word of the rainbow cloud of bubbles spread. Soon, the parking lot was filled with children chasing bubbles, popping bubbles, and laughing.

Lane watched as Fatima's daughter started it. An ululating cry — a sound Arthur called the *zaghruta*. Soon more women joined. An ululating chorus rose up with the bubbles. It was a wild wolf-like call — raw and untamed. A song of celebration.

×

Lane and Nigel sat in the interrogation room across the table from Donna and Stacie, whose red leather jacket was draped across the back of her chair.

Lane asked, "What can you tell us about John A. Jones?"

"Who?" Stacie asked.

"He's that guy from up north who's going to war with the oil companies," Donna said.

"You know him, then," Lane said.

"Know of him." Donna looked at her mother.

"What are you trying to get at?" Stacie began to frown as she looked into a compact mirror and used a tissue to wipe at the smudged mascara below her eyes.

"John A. Jones was killed in an explosion on the west side of the city shortly before your bubble machines went into action," Lane said.

Stacie's face turned red as she put the mirror away. "Are you accusing my daughter of being involved with him?"

"Hang on, Mom." Donna put her hand on her mother's arm. "He has to ask his questions. I know this guy. He's got a job to do. Remember, he could have cuffed us. I didn't stop when I was supposed to. He's being more than fair with us."

Stacie shook her finger at Lane. "You'd better not hurt my daughter!"

Lane wanted to smile. He looked at Nigel, who was covering his mouth with his right hand. Lane continued. "There was the potential for a massive loss of life if Jones's attack was successful. And we need to know exactly what happened and who was involved."

"Donna wasn't involved with this Jones fellow!" Stacie turned to her daughter. "Were you?"

"No." Donna turned to face Lane. "Today is the anniversary of my sister's death. I saw things escalating in my neighbourhood. Islamophobia has become a problem. You must have seen some of the signs. I thought maybe the bubble machines would calm things down."

"What was the glycerine used for?" Lane asked.

"When you mix glycerine and soap, you get better bubbles. Everybody knows that!" Stacie shook her head like she'd shared information that every other person on the planet but Lane was aware of.

"Glycerine can also be used to make nitroglycerine," Nigel said.

"The explosive that blew up a pickup and left a crater in the road just west of the city," Lane said.

"We know nothing about that." Donna looked at Lane.

"Are you saying we blew up a truck?" Stacie asked.

Lane looked at Donna, who smiled, shrugged her shoulders, and shook her head.

Nigel asked, "We're giving you the opportunity to admit your involvement in the explosion."

"Are you out of your fuckin' mind?" Stacie asked.

Lane and Nigel stared at Stacie.

Donna said, "Mom, please remember that you teach kindergarten."

Stacie looked at Nigel. "My daughter Lisa was killed by a bomb. We know what it's like to lose someone that way. Why would we ever do that to someone else?"

Lane thought, *Good point.*

Nigel looked at Lane for direction.

"Are you going to charge us with making bubbles?" Stacie laced the sentence with a sweet layer of sarcasm.

"Mom. I think they're trying to help. They used their lights to get us through the red light so we wouldn't get into an accident. They got the other officers to call off the chase. Maybe we should just answer the questions."

Stacie looked at Lane. "It was you who called off the chase?"

Lane nodded.

Stacie looked at Nigel. "You could learn a thing or two from him. The way you talk to women, I bet it's really hard for you to get laid."

"Mom!"

Nigel turned red.

Lane looked at Stacie. "Detective Li is my partner. I would appreciate it if you'd treat him with respect."

"I would . . ." Stacie began to say.

"And we could do without the sarcasm," Lane said.

Donna put her hand over her mother's mouth. "We had nothing to do with John A. Jones. In fact, what you're telling us about Jones is news to us."

Stacie pushed her daughter's hand away.

Donna said, "What are we going to be charged with? Failure to stop for a police officer?"

Lane looked at Nigel before he said, "Failure to stop for a red light."

"Oh," Donna said.

"Is that all?" Stacie asked.

"What other charges did you have in mind, Ms. Laughton?" Lane looked at Stacie and waited to see what she would say next.

Stacie looked at her daughter. Donna raised her eyebrows.

Lane started to laugh. *Where did that come from?* All of the tension of the last few days drained away. Tears came to his eyes. He saw the shocked silence on Stacie's face. He began to laugh harder. He felt Nigel's hand on his back. Lane surrendered as the laughter shook his body from paws to tail.

×

Keely stood and watched Chris Jones on closed-circuit television. She held her elbows with her crossed hands.

"What's the son been up to?" Lane asked.

Nigel followed him into the observation room.

"Not much of anything. He just sits there. He appears to be resigned to whatever happens next. It's like he's used to being controlled," Keely said.

"Any news on his father?" Lane asked.

Keely shook her head. "Fibre is on scene. He and his crew are picking up the pieces. It will take a DNA sample to confirm the identity. Apparently they've found a forearm, assorted bits and pieces, and precious little else."

"Are you okay?" Lane had another flashback of Jones's hand still attached to the steering wheel of the pickup truck.

Keely shrugged. "It appears that the bomber was the only fatality. We prevented a massive loss of life. I should feel happy. Then I look at this Chris kid, and I don't know what to feel."

Lane nodded and put his hand on her shoulder. "You two need some sleep before you can put this into perspective. I want you both to get some rest."

"After the interview," Keely said.

"I'll go in there alone for now," Lane said.

"One thing." Keely reached out to Lane. "In the car, on the way down here, he told the arresting officers he felt free."

Lane nodded. *Of course he does.*

Lane walked down the hall and opened the door to the interrogation room.

Chris sat in the corner wearing his camouflage pants and green T-shirt. The room stank of sweat and unwashed clothing.

"I'm Detective Lane." He sat down in the opposite corner of the room. Chris looked at Lane and nodded.

"I'm here to ask you some questions. Our conversation is being recorded. I need to remind you that you don't have to talk with me. You are entitled to the advice of a lawyer," Lane said.

Chris looked at Lane with clear blue eyes. He rubbed the top of his nearly bald head. "No, thanks."

Lane saw strands of blond hair on Chris's shoulders. "Who cut your hair?"

"My dad."

His voice sounds remarkably calm, almost disconnected. "How come he cut your hair?"

"He said I needed to get rid of the earring, and the haircut would help me to find humility," Chris said.

"How did you get the sulphuric acid?"

"Just checked the yellow pages for a place that did chrome plating, broke in, and took it. You'd be surprised what you can get into with a pair of bolt cutters."

"Who taught you how to do a B and E?" Lane asked.

Chris shrugged. "My father. He said it was part of my revolutionary training. He thought he was the reincarnation of John A. Macdonald and it was his job to start a revolt that would lead to a true Aryan Canada. He made me memorize John A.'s speeches about the supremacy of the white race."

"What about the nitric acid?"

"Took about a litre every night I worked at Foothills," Chris said.

Lane looked at Chris, who appeared to be studying the detective as if expecting more violent reactions instead of the respect he was getting. *He's probably used to being talked at and having the shit beat out of him if he shares an opposing opinion. Just keep asking the questions.* "Who hired Oscar Mendes?"

Chris looked at the floor. "I did."

"Where did Oscar die?"

"At the house." Chris appeared to study his shoes. He reached down to adjust the laces.

"Are you referring to your father's house near Lac La Biche?"

Chris nodded.

"How did he die?" Lane asked.

"Oscar figured out we were getting him to weld a container for the bomb, and he tried to run away. My father shot him."

"How did the body end up in a basement in this city?"

"My father told me to bring Oscar's body here. To hide it so that it wouldn't be found. I looked for a house under construction and buried him in the basement."

I wonder how you felt about that. "The girl who was killed on your father's property was killed with the same rifle?"

"He shot her too. The kids from town used to come out to the house on the weekends. They'd drive into the yard late at night. Dad got mad one Saturday night. Two pickups were roaring around the yard. One of the trucks kept backfiring. The little ones in our house started to cry. My dad took his rifle and shot at one of the trucks. He told us he had the right to defend his family and his property. Then he told us to keep our mouths shut."

His voice sounds resigned. "The officers who drove you here reported that you said you feel free now."

Chris lifted his head and looked at Lane. "My father controlled our lives. He told my mother she didn't need chemo after the doctors recommended it. He said it was poison. Then she died of cancer. My father said it was the will of God."

"You think differently?" Lane asked.

"I think my mother died because she did what my father said. Oscar died because I did what my father said. Oscar was kind to me. I'd never had a friend like him before. My father shot him in the back. My father died because he wouldn't listen to me when I tried to explain how unstable nitroglycerine is when the temperature rises. I should feel sad, but I don't. And I don't have to lie for him anymore. It's a relief."

"How were Donna and Stacie Laughton involved with you and your father?" Lane worked at keeping his voice neutral.

"Who?" Chris looked directly at Lane. For the first time, the young man looked confused.

"Donna and Stacie Laughton. The other members of your team."

"Team? My dad was paranoid. I was the only one who knew about the bomb. He wouldn't have told anyone else, and I never told anyone. My father killed Oscar because he was so paranoid about the oil companies and the government, because he thought Oscar was an informant. My father would never work with someone else. Especially someone he didn't know." Chris stared at the wall behind Lane.

"You're going to need a lawyer. I think that's the next step you need to take."

Chris shrugged. "Whatever you think."

Lane stood up.

"There's one other thing."

At that moment Lane felt as if he were in a church confessional. The impulse to shut off the camera almost overpowered all of his training.

Chris began to talk with his head down, his eyes focused on the floor. "I could have plugged in the auxiliary refrigeration unit. I knew that the nitro would become unstable very quickly as its temperature rose. But I didn't connect it. I didn't want to see anyone else killed. I saw the girl get shot. I saw the blood spray against the inside of the windshield. I saw Oscar after he was shot in the back. It took him fifteen minutes to die. He was screaming. I couldn't understand what he was saying because he spoke in Spanish. He kept coughing up blood. His eyes went out of focus. It was horrible." Chris lifted his head and looked at Lane. "I didn't want anyone else to die."

If you hadn't done what you did, I would have had to shoot your father, Lane thought.

Five minutes later, Lane walked into the observation room. Keely and Nigel looked up at him.

"Go and get some sleep. Chris is going to be fed and put in a cell. I'm going to send Donna and Stacie home. Agreed?" Lane asked.

"Please do it soon," Keely said.

"I'm with Keely," Nigel said.

"What happened?" Lane asked.

Keely said, "They've been fighting since you left them. We got a call from Lori. Stacie is driving her crazy."

"We made a deal. The interview is over for now. The two of you will go and get some rest. I'll take care of Stacie and Donna." Lane crossed his arms and waited.

"Is that an order?" Nigel smiled but couldn't hold onto it.

"Yes," Lane said.

"Thank God," Keely said.

Lane watched them walk away, then made his way back to his office. When he walked through the door, he studied Lori's face. She rolled her eyes and dipped her cowboy hat in the direction of the conference room.

He took a deep breath and opened the door. Lane was greeted by silence, the scent of new leather, and estrogen-laden air. *The atmosphere in here is electric.*

Both women looked at Lane but avoided eye contact with one another.

"Gather up your stuff. At this point, we have no further questions." He held the door, waited, and looked at Lori.

She mouthed the words *Thank you.*

"Can I call for a taxi?" Donna asked.

"I'm going home. If you like, I can give you a lift," Lane said and then thought, *This could be a huge mistake.*

"That would be great," Donna said.

Stacie picked up her helmet and jacket and steamed out of the room.

"This way." Lane turned right and headed for the parking lot.

Downtown traffic was heavy, and it took them fifteen minutes to leave the canyon-like streets and reach the open expanses of Crowchild Trail. The women in the back seat of the Chev sat on opposite sides and did not speak until they passed the lush university grounds and three cars of the LRT rolling on rails to their left. Lane looked up and saw a child with its finger in its nose. The child pulled its finger out, looked down at Lane, and wiped his finger on the window.

Stacie turned to Donna. "You know, you were close to your father and to Lisa. I always felt like an outsider. I was hoping one day we might become closer. That's why I wanted to come with you today."

Lane kept his eyes on the traffic and his ears open.

"It would be nice to be closer. We're the only ones left of our family." Donna watched the people in the LRT and their vacant stares.

"I know that I say stupid shit. Your father used to say my mouth was always in motion before my brain was in gear. I'm sorry." Stacie looked out the other window where all manner of home décor retailers lined the far side of a parking lot.

"I was going to ask for your help," Donna said.

Stacie turned to her daughter. "For what?"

"I have a lot to say, so could you just listen and not interrupt me while I try to explain?" Donna asked.

"I'll try."

"I have a friend. I've talked with him and his wife. I think he's going to agree to be the father of my child."

"You mean a turkey-baster dad?" Stacie covered her mouth with her hand.

Lane resisted the urge to look in the rear-view mirror. He kept his eyes on the road and carried on listening.

Donna took a long breath. "I've been looking at pamphlets for fertility clinics. The procedure is called artificial insemination. Since my marriage was such a disaster, I wanted to choose a father I know is a good man. This man and his wife — their names are Del and Susan — are good people. They told me they can't just walk away from the baby, so I've asked them to be godparents." She waited, expecting her mother to have something to say before she continued. "I've saved up money, the house is paid off, but I'll need help with the baby. I figure I can take six months off during the winter, but then I'll need someone to care for the baby while I keep the business going."

"And?"

"I was going to ask you if you would help me out with taking care of the baby, especially when I have to go to work." Donna continued to look out the window. The LRT slowed to stop at Dalhousie station and disappeared from view. She turned to her mother. "Well? What do you say?"

"I can't think of anything I'd rather do. Will you sell that damned motorcycle? It scares the hell out of me." Stacie lifted her helmet off the seat for effect.

"No, I was thinking of getting a sidecar for the baby."
Donna began to laugh.

×

Lane sat on the deck where the late afternoon sun was magnified by siding and glass to bake him and the dogs. Scout slept in the shade under the table. Roz sat in a smaller patch of shadow next to Lane. He sipped a cup of coffee and closed his eyes.

The gate opened. Lane looked to his right. Maria pretended to knock on her side of the fence.

"Would you like a cup of coffee?" Lane stood up, opened his gate, and waited for Maria to make her way across the concrete pad of their driveway.

"I would, but —" she rubbed her belly "— this one would start doing gymnastics after the caffeine."

"Water?" He pulled out a chair for her.

"Please." She sat down.

A few minutes later, Lane returned with a tumbler of ice water and a bowl of fresh strawberries.

"How did you know I've been craving these?" Maria picked up a berry, took a bite, and smiled.

Lane tapped his nose. "I know things."

"Like being right there this morning when that truck blew up?" Maria watched for a reaction.

"Yes, things like that." Lane reached for his coffee.

"And the two vans that started blowing bubbles. The latest story on that one is it marked the anniversary of the death of a medic in Afghanistan." Maria popped another strawberry in her mouth.

"The news is accurate for a change — at least about the bubbles," Lane said.

"And the bomb?" Maria asked.

Lane recognized the fear in her eyes, saw her glance at

her womb. "One fatality. The bomber, instead of innocents — for a change."

"What do you get out of all of this? Why do you keep doing your job?" Maria asked.

Lane looked at her. "It's the intangibles. Arthur is safe, Matt is safe, Christine is safe, Dan is safe, their baby is safe, you're safe." He pointed at her belly. "The little one is safe."

She stared at him.

"I'm sorry. I've said too much. Did I frighten you?"

She shook her head.

He wiped at his eyes and looked dumbly at the back of his hand where the moisture gathered in the hairs closer to his wrist. The tension that had gripped him for more than a week flowed out. *First I can't stop laughing, and now this.*

"You want me to freshen up your coffee?" Maria asked.

Lane nodded. "That would be nice." Her heard her get up. Roz licked the salty tears on the back of his right hand.

Following the older dog's example, Scout licked Lane's left hand and looked puzzled.

A car door slammed. Both dogs jumped up and scrambled to look through the chain-link fence. The front door opened. Footsteps sounded inside the house.

"Maria?" Christine asked.

"Just getting a coffee for Lane," Maria said.

"You're pregnant. Tell him to get his own damn coffee!"

Lane smiled as he used both hands to wipe away his tears.

"Hey! Your uncle helped save some lives today. So I'm getting him a cup of coffee to say thank you. Just tell me how he likes it."

Thirty seconds later, Christine opened the door. "You okay? Why are you crying?"

Maria followed and with her free hand tapped Christine's belly. "I hear congratulations are in order." She set the coffee down across from Lane.

"You told her?" Christine stared at Lane, hands on her hips.

"He sounded pretty happy about it, too." Maria sat down and took a sip of water.

"You are?" Christine looked confused.

Lane nodded, sipped his coffee, and tried to focus on Christine's reaction even though his vision was distorted. His voice wavered. "Why wouldn't I be thrilled?"

"I'm not married." Christine sat down.

Lane thought, *Here it comes. Just be quiet and listen.*

"The doctor put me on a different pill and . . ." Christine began, then thought better of it.

I don't need to know all of the details!

"I'm worried what my mom will say and do when she finds out." Christine looked down and saw that Maria was holding her hand. "And I'll have to quit school."

Lane shook his head.

"What?" Christine wiped tears away. Mascara stained the tips of her fingers.

"I think your Uncle Arthur wants to take care of the baby while you finish school. Matt is excited about being an uncle. What about Daniel? What does he think?" Lane asked.

"He's worried about telling his parents." Christine hesitated as she wiped her hands on her slacks. "What are you thinking now?"

"I'm thinking that in a few months there will be two new babies in the neighbourhood and it's gonna be interesting." Lane reached for his coffee. "And I can't wait to find out whether your baby is a boy or a girl."

×

Arthur found Lane later that evening. He was sitting with the dogs on the deck in the backyard. The heat of the day was waning, the sun cast long shadows, and the siding on Maria's house played a crackling number as it cooled. Arthur opened the door to the kitchen. "Got time for a beer?"

Lane looked over his shoulder, smiled, nodded, and took his feet off the plastic deck chair.

Arthur backed out the kitchen door, then down two steps to the wooden deck.

Lane got up and closed the door.

"The kids went to a movie. And we need to talk." Arthur set two beer glasses down and beside each glass a bottle of Moosehead beer.

Lane saw that both glasses were frosted from being in the freezer. *He's been planning this for at least a couple of hours. Before the kids came along this was a regular summer ritual.*

Scout cocked his head to one side as if he were trying to comprehend the conversation. He'd clearly picked up on the tension.

Arthur sat down in the chair next to Lane. He grabbed a glass in one hand and the Moosehead in the other. He tipped the glass and poured his beer so there would be less froth.

Lane reached for his glass and beer to do the same. He watched the bubbles erupt at the bottom of the glass. *It's all about the bubbles.*

Arthur took a satisfied sip. "Are you ready for this?"

"Ready for what?" Lane took a taste and felt the sharp, sweet taste of the barley bubbles on his tongue.

"The baby, the way it will change everything again. We've been through a lot the last few years, and I'm wondering whether we're ready for what's coming." Arthur leaned forward and set his beer glass on the table.

Lane looked at the top of the evergreen in Maria's yard. The sun backlit the top and it turned the dark green into emerald. "What exactly are you worried about?"

"How we'll handle it." Arthur took another sip.

Lane stared at the bubbles rising in amber. *Let him get it out. He's kind of like Scout the way he always circles a spot before he decides to settle down to sleep.*

"Christine is going to have a baby." Arthur looked at Lane. Lane raised his eyebrows and rolled his eyes.

"Don't look at me like that! You know I hate that! It's just that I finally think I'm not going to die right away —"

The circle is getting smaller now. He's getting closer.

"— and you know what she's like. She rides an emotional roller coaster on the best of days. Being pregnant will make her even more emotional." He looked at Lane.

Just let him circle once more. He'll get there. Lane continued to be mesmerized by the rising bubbles in the beer.

"I'm excited about the baby. But I'm worried." Arthur reached for his beer and took a sip.

Almost there.

"I wonder if you and I will make it. For a while I thought you didn't love me anymore. The baby will put a strain on our relationship." Arthur used his forefinger to point at Lane and then himself.

Just say it! "Are you over being a cancer victim?"

A V appeared in Arthur's forehead just below what used to be his hairline.

Watch out! You were way too blunt, as usual, Lane thought.

"I told you! I don't feel like I'm going to die right away. At least not today."

"Then things are getting back to normal?" Lane smiled.

"About as normal as things ever get around here." Arthur tipped his glass and drained it.

"We'll handle it. All of it. I know Christine will ride a roller coaster and expect us all to come along. I know there will be long nights, shitty diapers, and puke. But it will be fun." He lifted his glass and looked at the bubbles that were backlit by the evening sun. "Except for the puke."

Arthur shook his head, covered his mouth, and belched. "I just hope that we'll be okay."

"You want a fucking guarantee?" *Where the hell did that come from?*

"As a matter of fact, I do. And I want one from you." He pointed his finger at Lane and waited.

"What are you saying?" Lane shook his head at an inexplicable vision of champagne bubbles.

"Do I have to draw you a picture?" Arthur stood up, took his glass, opened the door, stepped into the kitchen, and slammed the door.

Lane's phone rang about ninety minutes later. The TV was on. Arthur was on the couch and snoring while a celebrity danced the rumba on the wide screen.

Lane went upstairs, found his cell on the kitchen table, and recognized Harper's private number. "What's up, Cam?"

"Got a minute?" Harper asked.

"Go ahead." Lane looked around the kitchen, then walked into the living room and sat in the leather easy chair.

"Do you think there's any reason to charge the Laughtons?" Cam asked.

"You mean besides the traffic offence?" Lane felt the leather warming to the temperature of his back.

"We're getting some pressure from a few concerned citizens who are reacting quite strongly to Donna Laughton's demonstration."

Now you're talking in riddles too. Just get to the point! "So you're telling me that Laura Poulin has been made to look the fool and she's looking for a scapegoat."

"Something like that," Harper said.

"Let's see. She wants the sister of a war hero to get some negative headlines. Then people will forget how Poulin tried to exacerbate a situation and Laughton diffused it." Lane heard a car door close outside.

"You understand that she didn't call directly, but there's a lineup of her political friends asking for appointments with Simpson." Cam used a tone that revealed more about Poulin's machinations than he probably would have admitted to anyone but his old partner.

"The only thing Donna Laughton is guilty of is great timing. She found a peaceful way of dialing down the emotions after the honour killing. It's not her fault a zealot attempted mass murder at the same time. It made Poulin look bad. She's connected in people's minds to the same tactics Jones used." Lane felt his anger rising as his words provided the focus for a percolating frustration.

"If you're right, then it explains why Poulin's crowd is sounding so shrill."

"So you're not going to add to the charges against the Laughtons?" Lane asked.

"Fuck no! Last time I checked, making bubbles is not a danger to the public."

"What else?" Lane asked.

"You sure you want to keep working with Li? I know we asked you to take him, but let's face it, you were his last stop and . . ."

"Li is working out just fine."

"You're joking, right?"

Lane heard the disbelief in Harper's voice. *I know Nigel's sarcastic, and I know he thinks he's always right, but the fact is he was right.* "He's an asset, Cam."

"ASSet." Cam spelled it out.

"In each case, when he made an assessment, he was freakishly accurate. And his language skills were invaluable. You have to understand that he's the kind of person who thinks of something outrageous to say, steels himself not to say it, then says it anyway." *You've said too much again!*

There was a ten-second pause from Cam's end.

"You still there?"

"I'm worried he'll get you killed. He is so sure he's right all of the time that when he does get it wrong — and let's face it, we all get it wrong at some point — he'll get you into a situation where one or both of you will be in serious shit."

"Shit happens." Lane's eyebrows tried to meet in the middle. *What the hell is wrong with you? Why are you picking a fight with Cam?*

"Somebody crap in your cornflakes?"

The front door opened, and Christine stepped into the house, followed by Dan and Matt. Lane looked at Christine. She saw his face, frowned, and asked, "What's the matter?"

"You've got a houseful. Call me after your gang is settled." Cam hung up.

chapter 11

Lane stopped out front of Keely's downtown hotel. Traffic was light at seven in the morning. She heaved her bags into the back seat and climbed into the front.

He handed her a coffee. "Black."

"You remembered." She took the cup and a cautious sip.

"Glad to be going home?"

She looked at him as he pulled away and into the centre lane. "How did you know?"

"The look on your face." He headed for Memorial Drive where early-morning joggers would be collecting sweat between their glutes as they ran along both sides of the river.

"I miss Dylan. I like my job, especially after things worked out the way they did with this case. And it's beginning to feel like home." She looked out the window at a man pushing a shopping cart filled with a collage of bags and one oversized suitcase. Behind him rose the latest tallest building in town. It was a steel-and-glass wing-shaped structure soaring into the blue sky. "I still don't get that." She pointed at the contrasting portraits of poverty and wealth.

"Oil and money," Lane said in a voice free of the disgust he felt.

They drove east along the river valley, then north up the freeway to the airport.

Keely pulled the morning newspaper from the side of her voluminous purse. She tucked it between her seat and the console. "Be sure to read the paper with your morning coffee."

"Thank you for your work on this one. It would have been a disaster without your help."

Keely nodded and smiled. "The funny thing is that I can't wait to tell Dylan about the soap bubbles and the glycerine. Is this a crazy country or what?" She laughed.

"For the first time in my career I was hoping the cameras would show up to get a shot of those kids playing with the bubbles. It would have been a great image for the news." Lane smiled.

"I wish I'd been there to see that Muslim woman stop everything from getting out of hand. What was her name again?" Keely took a sip of coffee.

"Fatima."

"Can you find out her last name for me?" Keely checked to see that the lid was tight on her coffee.

"I'll see what I can do." Lane looked over his right shoulder, signalled, and eased into the next lane.

"She could turn out to be a valuable source if we have any problems in the future."

×

Sister and Mother of Afghanistan Medic Blow Bubbles

Lisa Laughton was a medic killed by a roadside bomb in Afghanistan. Her twin sister, Donna Laughton, and mother, Stacie Laughton, wanted to honour her memory.

"Things were getting pretty heated in my neighbourhood after the murder of Shafina Abdula. My sister died because people used violence to solve their differences. I wanted to show the community there's another option," says Donna.

Her solution was to modify two vans to blow bubbles near a pair of neighbourhood churches that were involved in a war of words.

Earlier in the week, MLA Laura Poulin encouraged three women to walk on a Quran as an act of protest. Since then, Poulin has declined to respond to requests to explain her actions, but released a statement that says, in part, "The liberal media have blown this act of free expression out of proportion. Why aren't the pundits looking into reports that radicals from the Islamic Centre defiled a Bible?"

Laughton says, "Poulin's actions only escalated a volatile situation. I hope the bubbles will encourage dialogue instead."

"So you read the article." Nigel sat across from Lane at the coffee shop in Kensington.

"I hope Donna is right about the bubbles getting people to talk," Lane said.

Nigel stood up. "You want another Rolo?"

"Sure." Lane reached into his pocket for money, but Nigel was already on his way to the counter. Lane's phone beeped. He saw he had an e-mail message from Fibre. It said, "DNA has yet to confirm that the remains are John A. Jones. However, ballistics confirms that his rifle was used in two murders."

Nigel returned with two cups of coffee and a pair of chocolate cookies the size of dessert plates.

Lane looked at the coffee and the cookies.

"A bit of a treat by way of celebration."

Lane could hear the nervousness in his partner's voice and decided to wait him out.

"So, what did you want to talk with me about?" Nigel fidgeted in his chair, then looked around the coffee shop to see whether he recognized anyone.

"Will you please relax?" Lane waited for eye contact.

"I'm worried. You're my last chance. I mean, Harper warned me you were my final stop. Then I pissed him off. I figured after this case was over he would want to turf me even though things worked out the way they did. I mean there was a fatality, but it was the bomber. It wasn't one hundred percent successful, but you know, I think you prevented a huge disaster." Nigel reached for his coffee.

"Are you on something?" Lane broke a piece off his cookie.

"No!" Nigel sat back with an open mouth.

"First off, I didn't prevent anything. We did what we did with the help of Keely, Harper, the Chief, Lori, Lacey, and a bunch of uniforms. Second, if I got another partner, then I would have to deal with Lori. You wouldn't let that happen to me, would you?" Lane sat back and popped the chunk of cookie into his mouth.

Nigel turned his head sideways and frowned at Lane. "Did you just say you still want to be my partner?"

Lane covered his mouth as he chewed the cookie. "If you'll have me."

Nigel sat back. "If I'll have you?"

Lane lifted his coffee, took a sip, and put the cup down. "If we're still partners, then we need to get in touch with Miguel and let him know that Oscar's killer is dead."

Nigel took out his phone and thumbed through a series of numbers. "Now?"

"As soon as I finish my coffee." Lane reached for his cup, picked up his spoon, and scooped up a serving of chocolate whipped cream floating atop the Rolo. He smiled as he put the cream in his mouth.

Twenty minutes later, Miguel arrived outside of Higher Ground with two other men. Lane watched them through the window. Miguel parked a red Ford pickup across the street. The three of them jaywalked and went up the stairs. Inside the coffee shop, the men nervously looked around the packed room until Lane stood up and waved them over. The five of them managed to gather around the pizza-pan sized table with chairs borrowed from other tables.

Lane studied the men's hands. All three had thick fingers and rough palms. One had lost a pair of fingernails, and the flesh underneath was dark purple. As they shook hands and Miguel introduced them, Lane felt the power of their work in their fingers.

"*Mucho gusto*." Lane used the one phrase Nigel had time to teach him before they met Enrique and Ernesto.

Miguel brought more coffee and sat down.

Lane began to speak softly in English while Nigel translated. "We have the weapon that killed Oscar, and we have testimony from a witness who told us who shot him." Lane waited while the men listened to Nigel's translation.

Miguel nodded.

"The man who killed Oscar died on Friday. We wanted you to know this so that you can inform Oscar's family."

After Nigel's translated, Enrique turned to Lane. "*Gracias.*" Lane nodded as Enrique continued to speak.

Nigel said, "Enrique is Oscar's cousin. He will pass the information on to the family."

Most of the rest of the conversation was lost to Lane as the men began to speak in rapid Spanish with Nigel.

Lane thought, *I need to get home soon. I haven't seen much of my family for more than a week.*

When he got home more than an hour later, there was a note on the table.

Gone shopping for a new queen-sized

bed for Christine and Dan.

Love, Arthur.

Roz and Scout sat on either side of him and looked up with take-me-for-a-walk eyes.

He looked at the phone. The red light told him there was a message waiting.

Roz went to the front door. Scout followed her. They sat there and looked at Lane. He went upstairs and changed into a pair of lightweight pants and a light nylon shirt. He shut off his phone and put it on top of the dresser.

When he got back downstairs, he got the dogs leashed up and pulled on a pair of sandals. He stepped out the front door, down the stairs, and onto the sidewalk. The afternoon sun warmed his shoulders and face. The dogs tugged on their leashes. He followed their lead for a couple of steps, pulled back on the leashes, and waited for them to walk next to him. Roz settled in alongside while Scout continued to strain against the leash.

Lane snapped the leash. Scout wheezed. He crouched low to the sidewalk and used his muffin-sized paws to grip the concrete. For the next three blocks, Lane tugged, then made Scout sit. The muscles at Lane's elbow began to burn.

Roz growled and snapped at Scout. The younger dog fell into step next to Lane.

He smiled.

"Hey!"

Lane looked left toward the voice. He spotted Donna waving at him from behind her gate. Lane stood next to the vans with For Sale signs on their windshields.

Roz sniffed the air.

Lane thought, *Man, I just wanted to go for a walk*.

"Can I offer you a cup of coffee and maybe some baklava?" Donna asked.

Lane lifted the leashes and frowned.

"Bring them along." She opened the gate.

Lane felt unaccountably anxious as he walked up the driveway, along the side yard, and through the open gate. He looked for a patch of shade where he could tie the dogs.

"This is Fatima." Donna pointed an open left hand at the woman who sat at the table on the tiled deck bordered by blue flowers. "She brought over some baklava."

"Lane." He recognized Fatima as the woman who had stopped the boys tearing up the Bible in front of the Islamic Centre. Her black hair was cut short with a hint of red that glinted in the sunlight. Her eyes looked at Lane. He got the impression that she was sizing him up. *Do I shake her hand?* he thought as he tried to remember the proper etiquette for greeting a Muslim woman. "You're not wearing the hijab?"

"I wear it only at church." She smiled and pointed at the table. "Try some baklava. I made it this morning. Mine is the best you'll ever taste."

"What do you take in your coffee?" Donna asked.

Lane looked at her and waited for someone to say *Get your own damn coffee.*

Donna smiled. "I'm not gonna fix it for you. I just need to know what to bring out. And don't expect me to get your coffee on a regular basis. This is a one-time offer."

"Milk and sugar, please." He eyed a shady spot near the fence, untangled the leashes, and tied the dogs at separate fence posts.

When he turned around, Donna set the coffee pot on a hot plate. Then she added an extra cup, a carton of milk, and a container of brown sugar. She smiled at Lane, nodded at the empty chair, and held out her hand. "Sit down."

Lane sat and studied the women while he inhaled the honey and almond aroma coming from the plate of baklava. He poured his coffee. "Anyone else?" Both women shook their heads. He put down the carafe before adding milk and sugar to his cup. He stirred and smiled at the colour of the coffee. He sipped and closed his eyes.

"This is a good neighbourhood?" Fatima's accent was flavoured with hints of Arabic, Spanish, and French.

Lane nodded. "I like it."

"Fatima just made an offer on the place across the street, saw the vans out front, and knocked on my door." Donna reached for a square of baklava, popped it in her mouth, covered it with her hand as she chewed, and glanced at Fatima. "That is so good."

Lane saw that both women had turned to observe him. He picked up a square, popped it in his mouth, and savoured the combination of delicate pastry, butter, honey, and almonds as it dissolved on his tongue. "Delicious!"

Fatima clapped her hands and smiled.

Donna sipped her coffee and closed her eyes.

You're a cop, sitting at a table with one woman you arrested and another who peacefully diffused a volatile situation. This could only happen in Canada.

"You have children?" Fatima asked.

Roz barked. Lane looked toward the gate.

They heard a pair of sandals slapping up the driveway. Christine asked, "What are you and Scout doing here, Roz?"

"Hi, Christine," Lane said.

Christine looked over the gate at the three of them and focused on Lane. "I was looking for you."

Donna waved her hand to beckon Christine. "Come on in. Want a cup of coffee?"

"And some baklava?" Fatima asked.

Christine opened the gate and closed it behind her.

Lane pointed around the table. "This is Donna, and this is Fatima. Christine."

Donna pulled back a fourth chair. "Coffee?"

"I'd better not." Christine sat and turned to Lane. "There was a message on the phone."

Lane's gut clenched as it reacted to the tension in Christine's voice.

"How many months pregnant are you?" Fatima asked.

Christine turned on Lane. "You told them?"

Lane shook his head. He noticed that both women looked at the empty ring finger of Christine's left hand.

"You are his wife?" Fatima asked.

"What?" Christine glared at Lane.

"Christine is my niece," Lane said.

"She lives with you?" Fatima asked.

"Yes." Lane looked at Christine to see if his answer would upset her.

Fatima turned to Christine. "Where is your mother?"

"In Paradise," Christine said.

"I'm sorry to hear that. When did she die?" Fatima asked.

Donna covered her mouth, her face turned red, and a sharp bark of laughter escaped. She dropped her hand, her mouth opened wide, and more laughter flowed as Fatima looked at her with shock and disbelief.

Lane turned and recognized the expression on Fatima's face. "Paradise is a polygamist community in the south of the province."

"Oh." Fatima nodded and began to smile.

"I'm sorry." Donna grinned, took a deep breath, and pointed at Lane. "It's just that you interrogated me the other day, and now you're being interrogated."

Christine touched her uncle's arm. "The phone message was from my mother."

Donna saw the look on Christine's face. Her smile disappeared.

"She said there's no way she's going to allow her grandchild to be brought up by a pair of homosexuals." Christine clamped her hand over her mouth. Her eyes looked first to Fatima and then to Donna.

Donna and Fatima looked at one another. Donna shrugged.

Fatima turned to Christine. "Go on."

Lane thought, *Well, Fatima, you wanted to know what kind of neighbourhood this is. You might as well know before you finalize the deal on the house.*

Christine asked, "What am I going to do?"

"How did she find out so soon?" Lane asked.

"I told one of my cousins about the baby." Christine frowned and shook her head.

Lane was caught in the unexpected silence of the moment. "What do you *want* to do?" He felt the eyes of the other women on him as he concentrated on his niece.

"Have the baby. Finish school. Get a place of my own with Dan." Christine waited for Lane's reaction.

"So who's stopping you?"

"Your sister wants to." Christine's eyes glanced at the baklava.

"She may want to. The fact is that she can't. Your age means you are legally entitled to make your own decisions. All she can do is scare you if you let her." Lane opened his hands to invite a reply.

"Will you help us?"

"Of course I will. And so will Arthur and Matt." It was his turn to frown.

Fatima tapped Christine on the elbow with the plate of baklava. "Go ahead. It was what I craved when I carried my daughter. Now it's her favorite."

Christine nicked a square, popped it in her mouth, and reached for another. "I'm so hungry."

"Here." Fatima set the plate down in front of Christine. "Your baby is telling you to eat some more."

Donna stood up. "What would you like to drink? How about some water?"

"Water would be great, please." Christine popped the second square in her mouth and reached for a third.

"There is one thing you can do for me," Lane said.

Christine turned to face him with her mouth full and her eyes wide.

Perfect timing. Her mouth is full, and she can't answer back. "I want you to stop changing the words on the sign at the Eagle's Nest Church."

Christine blushed.

"That was you?" Fatima asked.

"We wouldn't want you falling off a ladder in your condition." Lane smiled.

Christine put her hand over her mouth. "Who told you?"

"You and Dan did. The pair of you make too much noise when you take the ladder out of the shed at night." Lane reached for a piece of baklava and popped it in his mouth.

Fatima sat back. "So you are the one. Everyone at the Islamic Centre wondered who was changing the words."

"Can this be our little secret?" Lane asked.

Fatima nodded.

Donna returned with a tall glass of water and a bowl of fruit. "Dig in, girl."

"You're being very nice to me after I barged in here like a crazy person." Christine reached for an apple.

Donna pointed her finger at Christine. "I'm just returning a favour." She nodded in Lane's direction. "Besides, something tells me we're going to have lots to talk about in the near future. So take your uncle's advice, take care of the baby, and stay off that ladder."

ACKNOWLEDGMENTS

Doctors Wheeler and Shaker: thank you.

Again, thanks to Tony Bidulka and Wayne Gunn.

Thank you to John and Dave for the police procedural advice.

Thank you to Colin for the chemical engineering consultations in the Co-Op parking lot.

Mary, Alex, and Sebi: thanks for the Central Blends suggestions and feedback.

Paul, Matt, Tiiu, Natalie, Cathy, and Leslie: thanks for all that you do.

Karma, thank you for the Spanish translations.

Thanks to creative writers at Nickle, Bowness, Lord Beaverbrook, Alternative, Forest Lawn, and Queen Elizabeth.

Thank you to Stephen of Sage Innovations (www.garryryan.ca).

Thank you to the people who run independent bookstores like Pages Books and Owl's Nest Books in Calgary.

Sharon, Karma, Ben, Luke, Indiana, and Ella: thank you for your love and support.

Garry Ryan lives in Calgary, Alberta. He received a B.Ed. and a diploma in Educational Psychology from the University of Calgary, and taught English and Creative Writing to junior high and high school students until his retirement. The sixth Detective Lane mystery, *Foxed*, was published by NeWest Press in 2013.